The Messes We Make of Our Lives

The Messes We
Make of Our Lives

The Messes We Make of Our Lives

Stories

Lowell Mick White

Buffalo Times Press

AUSTIN

Cover Art: *U.S. Department of Transportation Locomotive-Automobile Impact Test*
Author Photograph: Reji Thomas
Book Design: BTP

Buffalo Times Press is an imprint of **Alamo Bay Press**

Alamo Bay Press
Pamela Booton, Director
Lowell Mick White, Editor
Diane Wilson, Activist

For orders and information:
Alamo Bay Press
825 W 11th Ste 114
Austin, Texas 78701
pam@alamobaypress.com
www.alamobaypress.com

Publisher's Cataloging-In-Publication Data

Names: White, Lowell Mick, 1958-

Title: The messes we make of our lives : stories / by Lowell Mick White.

Description: Austin, Texas : Alamo Bay Press, [2017]

Identifiers: LCCN 2017900033 | ISBN 978-1-943306-06-0

Subjects: LCSH: Errors--Fiction. | Conduct of life--Fiction. | West (U.S.)--Fiction. | Texas--Fiction. | LCGFT: Short stories.

Classification: LCC PS3623.H57865 M47 2017 | DDC 813/.6--dc23

For

Wende Hilsenrod

and

Teri Sink

It's not the tragedies that kill us, it's the messes.
—Dorothy Parker

The Messes We Make of Our Lives

The Messes We
Make of Our Lives

The Road Back to Destruction Bay

All this began at a time when I was trapped, trapped in the hospital, trapped not just by ill health but by poverty, too. I was trapped, and there was no place for me to go. I slept during the day, so that I would not have to talk to anyone, and I sat alone in the dark at night, thinking of every place, any place, I had been and would now rather be, and every person I had ever known, people who had quickly come into my life and who were all now mostly gone.

I remembered a rainy morning leaving North Dakota, feeling depressed and very low, despite a giant shimmering cheerful rainbow stretching across the northern horizon. I drove all day west on Highway 2, into Montana, on the High Line, through patches of fog and drizzle, under more rainbows, past the white crosses that marked where people had died along the road. I drove west and my spirits—grew. There was a lot of empty space around me—signs of human presence, sure, but everything was very spread out and junky-looking. Cluttered. I liked it. In the afternoon I hit Havre, which seemed a mighty town after the emptiness of the plains. I stopped and had a beer at the Havre Daily Saloon, and years later that made me smile. The Havre Daily Saloon: not much of a bar, but I liked the name of the place—I liked the idea behind it. Thinking about it while I sat in the dark in the hospital made me happy.

*

The problem was, of course, that I was dying—dying not at the normal day-by-day rate we all die at, but much faster than I would have preferred had I given it any thought—and so one evening I had ended up in the emergency room, pierced by a badly-placed IV, listening to a man in the next alcove scream, "Oh God! Ohhhhhh! Ohhhhhh!"

Two youngish doctors—interns, residents, whatever—stood next to me, a man and a woman. The man appeared to be from South Asia, the woman from Latin America. They just stared at me with their flat brown eyes.

The screaming man beyond the curtain kept screaming. "Ohhhhhhh God! Ahhhhhhhhhh!"

Finally the man said, "No one's done his rectal exam yet."

He was looking at me.

I was dying, right?

Who cared about my rectal exam?

I didn't.

The woman was looking at me, too. She shook her head. She said, "No."

I looked up at the ceiling, dying wondering if it would be the last thing I saw. Bright lights, Fluorescent. The top of a pale green curtain shutting my gurney off from the screaming man and the rest of the room.

I thought, Well, this is it.

The end!

"Ahhhhhhhhhh! God! God!"

I thought, Goodbye!

The male doctor took a step back from my gurney. He said, "You do it."

Then he quickly ducked away beyond the curtain.

The female doctor frowned. I could see that she was pissed off—pissed at me, for some reason, like it was my fault. After a moment she said to me, "Roll to your side." When I did the badly placed IV yanked on my arm and I yelped. I tried to show my arm to the doctor, but she said, "Just lie still," and then she rammed her finger up my ass.

I realized then that while I might be dying a bit faster than normal, I wasn't yet dead—not yet, not yet.

✴

The next day I was wheeled into a room that looked out over the morgue.

"They're trying to send me a message," I said to Katy, my sometime girlfriend.

Katy said, "Oh, bullshit."

To a nurse I said, "This is awfully convenient—you all can just toss me out the goddamn window when you have a need to."

The nurse said, "We're going to make sure that's not going to happen."

I was unconvinced, but at the same time I knew that I was pretty lucky to be there. I was so miserably poor—I probably made a total of around $7500 that year—that I qualified for the county's medical assistance plan, and had better medical care than I might even have had with most regular types of health insurance. Without being so poor, I might really have ended up in the morgue rather than looking out at it.

✴

I shared my room at the hospital with a guy who had brain-damage and some sort of heart trouble. He was in his late thirties, maybe, and quiet, but his mother sat with him always and though I guess she was a nice enough lady she was very talkative and she near drove me crazy. She talked enough for eight or ten people. The old lady drove Katy away the first day, and that was fine by me. Katy wanted to talk, and I didn't want to talk.

Hell, I didn't even want to listen.

To anybody.

✳

The deal with my health was this: I had somehow at some time developed atrial fibrillation, a heart rhythm problem, which left my heart pumping about maybe 70% of its normal volume. Then I came down with the flu, and my feeble heart couldn't keep the fluid from my lungs, and so I was dying—drowning, actually, though the doctors called it congestive heart failure. The doctors decided to try to get my normal rhythm back by lowering the heart rate, and then bringing it back up. At least, I think that was the idea. I only know I slept for most of two days. I remember drowsing up at one point, and Katy and my doctor were standing there.

"He should be up and walking around," Dr. Jamail said. He was a very serious young man from Pakistan. "Why isn't he walking around?"

Katy said, "Oh, he's just lazy."

✳

When I woke up again, the old lady was sitting there, talking to her son about baking pies while he looked out the window at the morgue. She saw that I was awake. She asked, "Don't you just love a good apple pie?"

"I dunno—I guess." I got out of bed, trailing a long tube from my IV, and stumbled stiffly to the bathroom. The nurses were jabbing me with shots of lasix, a diuretic, forcing fluid out of me, and my overfull and painful bladder was about the only thing that could rouse me from the induced stupor I was in.

When I finally staggered back out of the bathroom, the old lady said, "Cherry pies, too—I just love baking cherry pies. Wouldn't you love to have a piece of pie right now?"

I said, "No, not really."

The old lady said, "Aw, that's a shame."

A damn shame. Sure. Actually, I don't much care for pie. Some ribs would have been good, though. Some fried chicken. Beer. I pulled a pillow over my face and went back to sleep.

✱

I woke up in the night, in the dark, and it was very quiet. I liked that. The brain-damaged guy was awake, too, but he said very little. His bed was next to the window, and he was staring out, watching the comings and goings at the morgue.

"Here comes an ambulance," he said. "They're bringing one in."

I stumbled to the bathroom.

When I came out, he said, "There goes a hearse, taking one away."

I shut the curtain between our beds drawn so that I wouldn't have to watch him looking out the window. From my bed through the open door I could see a corner of the nurse's station, but it wasn't a very active place in the middle of the night. There was one hot-looking nurse—her name was Chrissy—and she spent most of her time talking to someone on the phone.

I went back to sleep.

✱

In the Hemingway story "Now I Lay Me," Nick Adams, wounded and in a hospital, is afraid of the dark and he is afraid of going to sleep—he is afraid of many things. To stay awake and pass the time, he re-fishes all of his favorite streams. I tried that. I tried pulling out everything I had internalized over the years—all the people I had known, everyone who had ever damaged me or helped me or even talked to me, all the places I had been. I tried living— or dying, maybe—like a Hemingway hero, re-fishing not just my favorite and best-loved and best-remembered rivers, but re-driving my favorite streets and roads, too, and re-drinking my favorite bars, and re-listening to all the stories people had told me—re-living all the things that had been a part of me and were all now nothing but me, and I escaped my poor health and my poverty and I got back out on the road, driving in the city, the country, the mountains, driving everywhere, getting away from everything by dropping my Self and becoming everything and everyone.

✳

So from Havre on that trip I headed west and north, out of Montana and into Canada, following the Rockies in Alberta and then crossing into British Columbia. Still north, my memories a blur of trees, rivers, mountains, rivers, mountains, trees, trees, more rivers, more mountains, more trees, more everything, until I came out into the Yukon. That was different. Or by that time I was different, maybe. I drove on west through a light rain until the sun came out on the shores of Kluane Lake. The water was full of glacial debris and reflected the sky—a metallic unearthly blue. I parked my truck and got out and looked at it for a long time, at the dwarfish stunted trees, the weird blue water, cold rocky mountains rising behind me. The place was called Destruction Bay, and I decided that I would go there when I died, my strange cold heaven.

✳

Unlike me, the brain-damaged guy wasn't lazy, and he got up and walked around a lot—often most of the night. He would go to the cafeteria and get food and bring it back to the room and watch the morgue and eat. It was kind of disgusting, but I was usually able to ignore him. One night, though, I was sprawled out on my back with a pillow over my face, fishing in my mind the Yellowstone River below Carbella, and I heard a crash. He dropped something, I guessed, and I tried to work the sound into my memory, though that memory, really, had been one of very subtle and soft sounds—the gentle sucking sound of the water, the plashes of the feeding trout and whitefish, and the clear hard sound of a horse on the far side of the river cropping grass (an indication of how truly silent the evening was, for the Yellowstone is a wide and powerful river). But there was a crash. I adjusted my memory— maybe it was a car wreck way back on the highway running north from the park.

Then there was another crash, a big one. It sounded like a whole table or chair going over. I sat up and pulled the pillow from my face. A choking sound came from the other side of the curtain that separated me from the brain-damaged guy. I asked, "Are you okay?" but there wasn't any answer. More choking sounds. I leaned over and pulled the curtain back and he was slumped against the wall, choking, and his table and chair were both overturned, and I stood there shocked and watched him fall over, too.

I shouted, "Hey!"

I reached around for buzzer to alert the nurses but I dropped it—then I managed to grab it and I pressed on the button. I couldn't tell if anything happened or not. I leaned back the other way and saw Chrissy the hot-looking nurse talking on the phone.

"Hey!" I shouted. "Hey! Get in here!"

I tried to get up but my IV was hopelessly tangled.

"Hey! Help!"

And finally I got someone's attention, and soon a crew of nurses were hovering around the poor guy, and soon after that he was on a gurney and wheeled away and I never saw him again. I overheard a couple of the nurses worrying that they were going to get in trouble for not paying attention or something. Later, just before daybreak, just before I fell asleep for real, Chrissy told me that he'd had a stroke but had not died.

The old lady, his mother, shook me on the shoulder and woke me up around mid-morning. I was dreaming something dark and I jolted awake and saw the old lady and I cringed back, scared.

The old lady was crying. She said, "I know you did all you could to help him, and I want to thank you."

Then she squeezed my hand, and then she shuffled off. I never saw her son again, and I never saw her again, either.

✺

In the night I went to the San Juan River, drove up there from Austin. It was December, on this trip, my first trip to the San Juan, and driving across the plains I could see a front pushing south, storm clouds towering up into the sky. I watched it all afternoon, then crossed into it just before Lubbock. The temperature dropped abruptly, and when I pulled into Littlefield, Texas, for the night, it began to snow. The next morning I drove on across New Mexico, out of the dusty snow and into drier country. Something about north-west New Mexico reminded me of my former home in West Virginia—something, despite the fact that West Virginia is lush and green and the land around the San Juan is parched red desert. Then I realized that everyone around me was poor—that was why it looked familiar.

The water of the San Juan is so cold, pouring out from beneath Navajo Dam, that it suppresses most of the mayflies and caddis flies that trout feed on. Instead it produced vast clouds of diptera, midges, tiny insects that hatch in such incredible numbers that the trout exist in incredible numbers as well. Trout feeding on midges don't suck them off the surface like they do mayflies or caddis flies, they take them just under the surface of the water in a rolling, porpoise-like movement. I had never fished midges before this trip and it took me a while to figure them out, standing waist deep in the cold water, silent, watching the fish roll while stray flakes of snow fell. I stood there for hours, days, trying to understand the technique, and later those hours and days were repeated in a near-reverie in the hospital in the night. Finally, I understood the fish, I understood the river, I understood the midges, and I caught fish. In my mind this went on and on and on, but instead of heading back to Austin after that trip, which is what I did in what had dimly passed for real life, I disengaged and headed north from the San Juan, and it was no longer winter, but summer, or autumn, or whatever time of year I wanted it to be, and I fished my way across Colorado, hitting the Delores, the Piedra, the Rio Conejos, the Grand, the White, the South Fork of the Platte, into Wyoming for the North Fork, over to the Green, the Popo Agie, up to the Snake, into Yellowstone, fishing across the great rivers of Montana—the Beaverhead, the Madison, the Gallatin, the Missouri below Coulter Dam, the Kootenai, and then into Alberta to fish the Crow's Nest and the Old Man. Sometimes the weather was sunny, and sometimes it was rainy, as I wished. I drove deserted highways, I chased antelope, honked my horn at coyotes, I slowed through small towns that might or might not be interesting, as I desired, and I stopped in bars to talk to people who might or might not be real. I went on and on and on and I didn't ever want to stop, ever. And so I didn't.

*

Though there was one place I never wanted to go back to: Destruction Bay. Thinking of it now frightened me—there was something chilling about the weird blue of Klaune Lake, that strange blue that never came through in my photographs but was so brilliant and alarming in my memory. So—chilling. The lake, the ice-covered mountains to the west, the slow caravans of creepy old people in RVs making their way to Alaska like noisy elephants, something about all of it was very oppressive. The place frightened me. In my mind I much preferred to go back to the Bighorns, say, where there were some beautiful and friendly creeks I could re-fish at my leisure. But after some time in the hospital I realized that even the act of deliberately not remembering Destruction Bay was a form of remembering it. The fact that it existed now as an unconscious void out there—somewhere on the edges of my mind—made it even more powerful.

*

I was alone in my room for about a day after the brain-damaged guy was wheeled away. Then they brought in some administrator from the university who was having a heart attack. He didn't say too much but still I resented him. I wanted to be alone.

The first afternoon he was there he created a commotion while I was asleep—he woke me up, yelling "He's dying! He's dying!"

It took me a moment to figure out that the heart attack guy was all excited about me—he thought I was dying. Apparently I snored and snored, and eventually I stopped breathing—then, gasping, lurched into trance-like lazy waking, then back to sleep and to more snoring. After some time Dr. Jamail arrived and announced that I probably had sleep apnea, and he had some technicians wheel in a C-PAP machine, a device that blows air down a sleeping person's throat to keep air passages open.

I quickly fell in love with the C-PAP—now not only could I sleep without choking or suffocating, without having the disturbing realization burst in on a dream that I was dying, dying, dying, suddenly knowing that I had to wake up immediately and breathe, I was able to truly sleep comfortably with a pillow over my face. I was able to sleep better, and better able to shut out the rest of the world. That first time as I went back to sleep I thought about snoring, snoring, about the summer in Montana when I went into Livingston and stayed in a motel for a few days after a couple of weeks of sleeping in the back of my truck. Saturday night I went out to a bar, and was flirting around with a of pair chunky, funny girls, sisters from Lethbridge, Alberta. They were having a good time except for the fact that the guy in the room next to theirs back at the motel was a snorer. A bad snorer! They banged on the walls, they told me, they banged on the door, and still the guy wouldn't wake up and stop snoring. He was ruining the trip! He was keeping them awake! They couldn't sleep! And as I listened to them, I slowly realized that they were complaining about—me....

✳

Now, though, with the C-PAP pumping air down my throat and a pillow over my face, I could drift off sleeping without snoring, without choking and dying, fishing in the days as well as the nights, and in my dreams I drove every highway I remembered fondly—Route 47 across central West Virginia, 298 along the Clark Fork of the Yellowstone in Wyoming, 89 down the front range of the Rockies in Montana, various backroads in Bighorn National Forest and Ocala National Forest, 118 in South Texas, 207 in the Panhandle, other roads whose numbers are lost to memory but remain nonetheless as images of sunlight or mountains or trees or clouds. I listened to music, I drank beer, yelled out the window at passing cattle, I stopped off in little country taverns for a beer or two before heading on, and on. Before I began dying and went into the hospital not only was I too sick to go anywhere, I was too poor as well. I was driving a cab, a hard way to make a skimpy living, stuck circling the town I lived in twelve hours a day, seven days a week. People would get in the car and sit behind me and tell me where to drive, and I drove—down South 1st to Ramble Lane and maybe around Sahara to Boxcar Run. You know where Boxcar Run is? I knew. I took people there. Then maybe north on Congress, across the river and through downtown, around the capital, north on Lamar to somewhere up there mysterious, and then south again, or north—Simarillion Trail and Frodo Cove, Arapaho Trail and Packsaddle Pass. Possum Trot. Aries Lane. I drove and I drove, and the people sat back out of sight behind me, I seldom saw them. They told me where to go, and they told me stories, too. And now, dying, or almost dying, on my hospital vacation, dreaming in the dark, dreaming awake or asleep, all these places and people came together in memory. The places I visited or even just drove by were all my places now, no matter who really lived there, and the people who told me things were all me, and all their stories were my stories now.

Deep Eddy

In the morning it was raining, and we ended up stuck behind a caravan of senior citizens, all in big recreational vehicles, all from Washington State, all heading south in the rain. I whipped on down the road, sliding in and out between the campers, and every time I passed someone I could feel Amanda tense up beside me on the seat. She was afraid of the big mining trucks that were heading north. Every time I pulled out to pass, she tapped the floor of the pickup with her right foot, searching for a brake pedal. I did my best to ignore her and drive, and so I drove and I drove, and I counted the RVs, 64 of them in all, I think, and I knew they must all be together because of the big red decals that each vehicle had on its rear. I drove on south, the windshield wipers thudded, and Amanda tapped the floor. Neither of us said anything. Once we got past Whitehorse, the rain stopped and traffic seemed to let up, and Amanda was able to relax a little and fall asleep.

How can you truly tell when someone's desperate?

I didn't see anything then. I didn't notice anything.

And if I had noticed something, would I have cared?

Amanda woke up sometime later when I pulled off the road, a small cloud of white dust blowing up and around us. When it cleared I could make out an overflowing red litter barrel and a tarnished length of guard rail, and, beyond that, a valley. A range of mountains rose on the other side of the valley, shaded by clouds. A motor home and a mining truck went by, heading west, north, blowing in more dust. Everything seemed dryer, though there were still some muddy puddles in the gravel.

Amanda frowned, still half asleep. "Are we there yet?"

"Those are the Cassiars over there, I think," I said. "And that's, I guess, the Rancheria River."

Amanda looked away at the mountains. She asked, "How much farther to Fort St. John?"

We stayed at a motel in Fort St. John on the way up: hot showers, clean sheets, firm mattresses, cable TV, wireless, cell phone reception, air conditioning.

"I don't know." I said. "Maybe 900 miles. We might make it by tomorrow if we push it."

Amanda rested her head against the window of the truck. The weak sunlight cast a shadow across her face.

She said, "Then let's push it."

I waited a moment. I asked, "You're not getting out?"

"No." Amanda sounded serious.

Oh, well. I was tired of her complaining, but I tried not to let it show. To hell with her. I shrugged and opened the truck door. I collected five bottles—three Labatt's and two Cokes—and a wad of paper from under the seat and carried it all over to the trash barrel and jammed it all in. The turnout was at a bend in the road at the top of a bluff. Below, beyond the guard rail and down the steep bluff, the Rancheria twisted through a wide marshy valley and disappeared off to the northwest. Cloud shadows scudded over the valley. The Cassiars were light gray. Cold-looking. Between the turnout and the mountains a single cloud was dropping rain, dark gray streaks that settled into the haze. A car with its headlights on went by, blowing dust, heading northwest to Whitehorse. Yukon plates.

I walked back to the truck and leaned in. I said, "I have to pee."

Amanda sighed. She didn't even open her eyes. She said, "That's fine."

✳

The slope of the bluff was steep and somewhat slippery. It was damp but not muddy, and was covered with hard pale gravels that rolled out from under my feet. I rested against a burned-out stump and caught my breath before sliding the rest of the way down the slope. At the bottom there was a fire ring made of gathered wild stones. Ashes, some beer bottles, and a half-burned throwaway diaper were in the ring. Logs had been rolled up close for seats. A path led down to the river.

Up on the bluff big truck of some sort headed south on the highway, and dust swirled in a cloud and drifted down the slope.

In the silence that followed the truck I heard the river. I buttoned my jeans and followed the path, scrambling over a deadfall and splashing across a little creek coming from the north. The creek disappeared into a thicket, but further ahead I caught a glimpse of open water. I climbed over another deadfall, ducked under some alders, and came out on the banks of the river.

The Rancheria came out of the southeast, headed toward the bluff, and turned suddenly to the west. It flowed past my feet and turned on into the south, dropped into a riffle, and disappeared behind some brush. At the base of the bluff, where it turned, there was a logjam and an eddy. The creek seemed to come in there. The water below was shallow and clear with a sandy bottom. Two smallish grayling cruised the base of the pool.

What pretty water, I thought. Look at those wild fish.

Those grayling have never seen a fly.

I am the first man to see them.
I discovered this spot.
Those fish are mine.

✺

When I got back to the truck, Amanda was counting the RVs. She had my clipboard and was making a mark every time one passed. Well. I got a beer out of the cooler and walked around to the driver's side and got in.

Amanda said, "You must've had to go pretty bad."

"Yeah, I was looking at the river." I twisted the top off the bottle and took a long drink. My jeans were wet from the knee down and there was a scratch on my face, but I didn't care. I said, "I saw this huge grayling. I want to see if I can catch it."

"Those old people from Seattle just passed us," Amanda said. She tilted the clipboard so I could see it—there were a lot of marks. "Most of them—maybe all of them. They blew dust on me."

"We'll pass 'em again," I said. "They drive slow."

"Yeah, and they'll slow us down."

"I'll go catch that fish and let 'em get ahead of us." I tried smiling at Amanda but she just stared at me.

"Look at this," Amanda said. Again she held up the clipboard with all the marks and slashes on it.

Okay, there were a lot of RVs on the road. I could see that. So Amanda could count.

"I'll just be a minute," I said.

"Come on," Amanda said. "You've caught enough fish already. Okay?"

I looked away and began digging through the pile of maps on the seat between us.

Amanda asked, "Okay?"

"No...." I found our battered copy of the Yukon guidebook and started thumbing through it. I looked up. "No, really, this grayling is enormous—first I saw two little ones, then I saw the big one. He's never seen a fly before. Nobody's seen him before. It's like a whole new world down there."

"Sure," Amanda said. "Right off the road."

"Yeah," I said. I thought of the fire ring and the diaper. Right. There were people here, somewhere, people came here, passed by here, stopped here, littered here—but there wasn't anyone here now, except me. So this was my spot. Mine. I discovered it. I was an explorer. I said, "Isn't that great?"

Amanda turned away from me and looked out the window. Two more clouds were dumping rain somewhere near the mountains.

I found our place in the guidebook and started to read. "'DC 663.4....' Hey, I was wrong. We're only about 600 miles from Fort St. John. Six-sixty-three from Dawson Creek."

Amanda still didn't look at me. She said "Well, let's get going."

"No, wait...." I said. I began reading again. "'DC 667—'"

"Four more miles already?"

"'DC 667...Litter barrel with view of the Rancheria River to south.' That's where we are."

"We have a GPS," Amanda said. "We already know where we are. So—let's go, okay?"

"No, wait...'Rancheria River, fair to good fishing for bull trout and grayling.' Well, I guess. The grayling are there, at least." I looked up. "You should see this grayling, it was huge—"

"There's no such thing as a huge grayling," Amanda said.

"It's bigger than any we saw in Alaska. Over 18 inches, easy."

Amanda shifted in her seat, turned to face me. She reached for my beer and took a sip, and made a face. It was warm. We were out of ice.

"Jon," she said, slowly. Choosing her words carefully. "I'm really tired. I'm even tired of looking at—trees. You know? Everything looks the same. We've driven something like eight thousand miles in the last—"

"Aw, no," I said. "C'mon. Really, it's more like about six thousand."

"Okay! So it's six fucking thousand. I don't really care. I just want to get to wherever it is we're going today, and I want that to be just a little closer to home than we are now. I mean, I guess—I don't know." She sighed. Very dramatic. She said, "Fuck."

I looked over at her and tried smiling again. I guess I was a phony, because I didn't care. I just smiled. I just showed my teeth. Phony. I even took her hand and squeezed it.

I said, "This is what I want to do. It'll just be a few minutes. This fish has never seen a fly before."

Amanda pulled her hand away. "You don't even keep the damn things."

"Catch and release," I said. "All the way."

I got out of the truck, shut the door, and leaned in the window.

"You want to get out and watch?"

"No!"

"Sure?"

"Yes, I'm damn well sure."

I took a step back. So she was pissed. So what. I had a right to do what I wanted to do, too. I stepped around to the back of the truck and looked at her through the layers of glass, and I thought of the trip out: prairies, plains, grasses, rivers, badlands, rivers, mountains, rivers, trees, rivers, trees, bridges, trucks, mountains, glaciers, more trees, more rivers, good roads, bad roads, old people in RVs—ten days from Austin to Anchorage, two weeks in Alaska, and now we were still at least a week away from home. She was tired, of course she was tired, and she was pissed off, too. But being tired and pissed off wasn't going to get us home any time sooner. I had a right to do what I wanted to do, and right now I wanted to go fishing.

I went back around to the window and said, "We'll get there fine."

"You know," Amanda said, "it would've been a whole lot easier if you'd just left me back in Whitehorse—then I could've caught a flight home and you could dick around in the woods and play fucking Lewis and Clark all you wanted."

"Aw, come on," I said. But I thought, To hell with her. So she was tired and pissed. "It'll be just a few minutes. Then I'll come back and drive like hell. We'll pass the old people. We'll make it fine."

Amanda said, "I don't think so."

I didn't say anything else—there wasn't anything to say, really. I walked around to the back of the truck again. I looked back at her and I saw her take another sip of warm beer, and I saw her twist the rearview mirror around to watch me. After that I ignored her. I dug around in my fishing gear, and I pulled out a rod, a fly box, some gadgets. When I looked up again I saw Amanda pour the rest of the beer out the window.

✳

When I got into place, the river came straight at me, and then turned, the main current curving toward the south and back into the east. I was a little off to the side of the eddy, where a small current circled around and around, out of the main river, burbling up against the bank, along the little sandbar the creek had deposited under the logjam, and back out into the main current of the river. It was pretty water, clear and cold, and it reflected the sky, the trees, me.

The water seemed pretty deep. I tried looking down through the reflective surface and even with polarized glasses could only see deep greenish shadows. This was probably the place where fish in this section of the river spent their winters, finning around under the ice and snow, holding in the dark, waiting for spring and breakup.

And I saw then the big grayling float up out of the green—I watched it get bigger and bigger, watched it suck down a bug, a grayish-tan caddis fly of some sort. The fish made a little slurping noise and settled back a foot or so in the water. Two other, smaller grayling appeared and hovered off to the left. They all could stay in the eddy as long as they wanted and the river would always swirl food right up to them.

And I thought, This is why I came on this trip in the first place—to see this, the river, the mountains, the ev-erything.

I thought, This is the way life is supposed to be, al-ways.

This place, this water, these fish. Everything new.

Yeah, I stood there watching those fish for a long time.

Then I took a breath.

I stood holding my fly rod with a little fly called an Adams, bushy and gray, tied at the end of the leader. I stepped to the side to put more of the bush between me and the fish. There wasn't much room to cast, but I didn't need to cast far. I worked out a little line and slop-rolled a cast into the eddy. The leader straightened out just enough and the fly dropped softly onto the water.

Nice, I thought. Grayling look up. They like to eat insects off the surface. Good. That Adams sort of looked like a caddis. Good, good.

I held my breath.

And then it was very easy. The eddy brought the fly to the big grayling, who spotted it, rose, finned back in the water for a second, looking at it, and then sucked it down.

I set the hook. The shocked grayling jumped, bored out to the main river, quickly jumped twice more, then again, and then tried to go deep. I was using a heavy leader, though, and I pressured the fish, keeping him near the surface of the eddy. One more jump.

It was very easy.

I knelt over the panicked fish and picked it up. It was slick and iridescent, gleaming in the sunlight, green and bronze, heavy and fat. It gasped in the air, trying to breathe. The big dorsal fin was swept down but I ran my finger along it, pulled it up. A big, big fin. I measured the fish against my rod, and it covered the writing right up to where it said 5 Weight—it was maybe 18 inches long, maybe 19 inches, easy 16 or 17, 20 inches if I ever felt like lying.

I tried to work fast. I took out my cell phone and took a quick picture of the fish, and then I removed the fly and got the grayling back in the water, holding it by the tail. In a minute or so the fish wriggled and I let go. It shot back into the eddy, into the shadows, and went deep.

I stood looking at the water—and it was then that I realized that back up on the bluff Amanda was leaning on the truck horn.

✳

And I guess I just missed her.

I climbed up the bluff, breathless, and got to the guard rail at the turnout, and she was gone. My truck was gone. There was a battered Chevy pickup with Yukon plates parked there, and an old fat guy with a big head of white hair and a gut spilling out between suspenders standing next to the truck—and there was the overflowing trash barrel, and some muddy puddles in the gravel with some of my stuff scattered around. But Amanda was gone, and my truck was gone.

I stood there breathing, trying to breathe, my fly rod pointed out behind me toward the river.

The fat guy said, "I guess you're the boyfriend."

Next to one of the puddles I saw a duffel bag that had

held a lot of my fishing gear, and the ice chest. Some of my clothes strewn around, too.

"She said you were down there fishing," the fat guy said. "She said you were maybe lost. I was thinking about going to go look for you."

"I wasn't lost," I said.

"Tourists get lost here all the time."

"I'm not a tourist," I said. "I'm an explorer."

"Well." The fat Canadian looked at me and thought about that. Finally, he said, "That gal was really mad."

I asked, "Yeah?"

I pulled out my cell phone to call Amanda, get her back here. No reception, of course. Useless. I put it back in my pocket.

"What're you fishing for?" the Canadian asked.

"Grayling..." I said. "Listen—did she say anything?"

"Just that you were fishing and maybe lost. And I could see she was mad."

She was mad. Yeah. Well, fuck that. I climbed over the guard rail and looked at my belongings. A big bag with my reels, and some fly boxes, and a pair of neoprene waders and boots. A pair of jeans and three or four heavy shirts tossed down on the gravel—one shirt with its sleeve trailing in a puddle. I stepped over and opened the ice chest: four Labatts, no ice.

And Amanda was mad.

Okay.

I took one of the beers and stepped over and leaned back against the guard rail. Opened the beer. The big Canadian was looking at me. The breeze ruffled his white hair. A pair of RVs headed south, close together, and dust rose up from the road. Behind me the river, the Cassiers.

"Well," the Canadian said. "I guess that gal just ran off and left you."

After the Unexpected Garage Sale I Decided to Move to Texas

It got hot sometimes where I lived then, on the edge of the plains, dry and hot, and the wind blowing all the time, and on those days it was good to have air conditioning. Even if it was just a window unit, it was good to have, and I could sit inside—our home—and be cool with Molly and the dogs. Everything, I thought, was fine. But all of a sudden I didn't have air conditioning any more—I didn't have Molly, or the dogs, and I didn't even have electricity, and I was left with nothing to do but sit back in the recliner, drink a cold beer from an ice chest, smoke a cigarette, and think about things. Think about—brood about, ponder about, cogitate about, wonder about—whatever the hell had just happened.

And that's when the air conditioner started to move.

It made a grinding sound, waggling up and down in the window. I looked at it for a moment, then got up out of the chair and went out on the front steps.

My neighbor—friend, I guess—Joe Sullivan, was standing there with his hands on the air conditioner.

"Oh, hey there," Sullivan said. "I thought you left."

He didn't look startled or even embarrassed, trying to

run off with my air conditioner.

"The lease here—" I said. Was canceled. It was hard to explain. I said, "I'm still around."

I sort of lifted my left hand for a beer, then realized that I'd left the beer—and the cigarette, too—sitting on the table next to the chair.

"Tell you what," Sullivan said. He was leaning on the air conditioner, squinting in the sunlight, crinkling his eyes at me. "I'll give you twenty-five bucks for it."

"What?"

"Twenty-five bucks for the air conditioner."

I blinked, squinted back at him, squinted past him at the street, the other houses, the hot pale late summer sky. Then I squinted back at him some more.

"Are you crazy? I just bought that new last May. It's only—" I stopped and tried to count. It was September, but I couldn't remember offhand how many months that was from May—five six, four, it seemed forever. "It's only a summer old."

"It's not running," he said. "It's busted."

"That's because the electric's turned off," I said.

Molly didn't pay the bill or something.

Molly didn't do a lot of things. But maybe she did.

"Okay, then," Sullivan said. "Fifty dollars."

"Maybe I'll need AC at my new place," I said. "Forget it."

I went back in the house and saw that the cigarette had rolled out of the ashtray somehow and was burning a hole in the filthy carpet, smoldering. I picked it up and poured some beer on the blackened burn spot and settled back into my chair and started staring some more at the wall. That's all I pretty much wanted to do. Then I heard a little tapping noise and looked up and saw Sullivan standing in the doorway.

"Can I come in?"

He came in before I could tell him No.

I said, "The air conditioner's not for sale."

"No," he said, "I just wanted to see how you were doing."

I shrugged and he walked on over and sat on the couch. The couch was in tatters, chewed to pieces by the dogs when Molly left them locked up in the house for two weeks while she was off with her boyfriend smoking crack or whatever she was doing.

Those poor damn dogs!

Locked up like that—no food, no water. Just a couch to chew on.

I thought Molly loved those dogs.

I looked at Sullivan, that poor damn couch all torn apart.

He was lucky a spring didn't screw him in the ass.

"That's a nice TV," Sullivan said. "Sony."

"It's not for sale, either," I said. The TV was mounted high enough on the wall that the dogs couldn't get to it.

"No, I was just thinking it was a nice TV." Sullivan took off his cap and ran his hand across his head, then put the cap back on. "Too bad you don't have electricity. We could watch the Chiefs."

Oh, I thought. This must be Sunday.

Tomorrow's Monday, then. I'll have to go to work.

Well, shit.

I looked over at Sullivan. He wasn't a bad guy, he was a neighbor, he was sort of a friend, he only wanted a cheap air conditioner.

"Want a beer?" I asked. I gestured at the blue plastic cooler next to the chair. "I stocked up."

"Sure." He got up and pulled a can out of the cooler and settled back onto the couch. He had only just sat down and already couch stuffing was sticking to his clothes.

"You talked to Molly?" he asked.

"Not since she left." Why would I want to talk to a crazy woman?

Sullivan shook his head and popped open the can of beer and took a long drink.

"The beer's cold," he said.

"I bought some ice, too," I said.

"Yeah," Sullivan said. "You know, I think Molly went kind of crazy while you were gone."

I nodded at that. "Yeah, I guess."

"Yeah," Sullivan said. "She went through some sort of manic phase."

Sullivan and his wife had dozens—maybe hundreds—of self-help books in their house. I was over there once and I stood staring at those shelves of books, shocked, wondering what they were good for. But apparently they were good for something, though, because Sullivan and his wife were still together and Molly and I weren't, and his wife was sane and Molly wasn't, and he had electricity and I didn't, and my house was all torn to shreds and his wasn't.

And also, yeah, Molly went fucking crazy or something.

There was a tap at the door and we looked up. The old lady from next door was standing there. Mrs. Borgan. She was a little old lady whose husband was retired from the post office.

"Hello, there!" she said. She sounded very cheerful, she was always very cheerful, and she looked at me and smiled. "I just came to see how you were doing."

"He's doing fine," Sullivan said. "He's really hanging in there."

I glanced sideways at Sullivan and sat up and pulled another beer from the cooler.

"Care for a beer?" I asked Mrs. Borgan.

"Oh, no, thank you," she said. She came on into the house and looked around. "Oh, my."

I sat back in the chair. Yeah. Oh fucking my. That's pretty much what our landlord had said, too, when he saw the place. I had only been back a day, not even a day, and was trying to figure out what the deal was with Molly—she was there when I got back, wild, and she drove away and drove back again, wilder, and the dogs were jumping around half-starved and crazed—when the landlord stopped by for an inspection. Someone, I guess, had tipped him off about the dogs. He took one look and said, "Oh, my" and then he told us to get the hell out. Molly said "Fine" and threw a few things together and gathered the dogs and got in her car and drove away. I hadn't seen her since.

"I didn't know things were this bad," Mrs. Borgan said. She wandered off into the kitchen, stepping carefully to avoid the piles of dog shit on the carpet.

I looked over at Sullivan and he shrugged.

"The Chiefs are pretty good this year," he said after a moment.

I thought about that for a long minute. Then I nodded and said, "Yeah."

We heard a noise in the kitchen and then Mrs. Borgan came through, pushing the microwave oven on a little cart.

"Molly said I could have this," she said. "Something to remember her by."

"She wanted you to have the microwave?"

"Uh-huh." Mrs. Borgan gave a little grunt as she pushed the cart from the kitchen linoleum up onto the carpet. The little wheels of the cart crushed a dog turd into the carpet but Mrs. Borgan didn't notice.

"Jesus," I said. "Why don't you just take a plant or something?" We had lots of plants around the house. They were all looking pretty sickly and battered since whatever had happened to Molly had happened.

"Why, thank you, Dan," she said cheerfully. She unhooked a big fern from the ceiling over by the blank television set and placed it unsteadily on top of the microwave.

I got up out of the chair.

"Listen, I can't let you take the oven," I said.

"Why not? Molly said I could have it."

I thought about that. I asked, "Have you talked to her recently?"

"No, but I remember she always said I could have this oven if something happened to her. She always loved my microwave roasted chicken, and this oven's so much better than mine—" she patted the oven "—and she said that if anything happened to her, she'd feel better knowing I had her oven. Every time I roast a chicken in it I'll think of her."

"I don't know for sure if anything happened to Molly," I said. "I haven't talked to her."

"She went crazy," Mrs. Borgan said. "Everybody says so."

Everybody said so.

"I'll have to talk to Molly first," I said. "When I do I'll ask her about the oven."

Mrs. Borgan stood there looking disappointed, sticking her lower lip out, pouting. She looked like a wrinkly little girl.

"You can keep the plant," I said. I handed it to her.

She looked at it doubtfully. She said, "It's kind of sick."

"I'm sure you can fix it." I looked around for something else to give her. I spotted a deer skull on the mantle over the fireplace. It had one antler—the left one—and had been bleached white by the sun. Molly and I had found it while hiking once in Big Bend National Park. I know there's some law against taking artifacts from national parks, but we took it anyway. I had always felt kind of guilty about having it. But now I reached over and took the skull off the mantle and handed it to her. Passing on my guilt.

"Molly would want you to have this," I said.

Mrs. Borgan looked at the skull closely, holding it by the antler. "Donnie might like it," she said. Donnie was her grandson.

"Molly always did like Donnie," I said. I guessed, I didn't know—who the hell knew what Molly liked or didn't like? I sure didn't.

I pulled another beer from the blue cooler and sank back into my chair. I glanced over at Sullivan. He was sitting quietly on the ruined couch, sipping his beer. I realized I'd have to give him something, too, now. But I'd be damned if I was going to give him my air conditioner. Not even for twenty-five dollars.

Mrs. Borgan stood holding the skull and the fern, looking around the room.

"It's so odd she left and didn't take her things. I watched her leave—she just threw her bag in the car and put those three big dogs in the back seat and off she drove."

"Yeah." I said. I hadn't really tried to stop her, either. Actually, by that time I was kind of scared of her. What can you do with a determined crazy woman? The landlord and I stood on the steps and watched her drive away. Molly drove down the street, made a u-turn, and came back. I thought maybe she'd come to her senses or something but all she did was get out of the car and take down a hummingbird feeder that was hanging from the sycamore. The dogs sat in the back of the car watching her. "I forgot this," she said, and then she got back in the car and drove off, and this time she didn't come back. I went back in the house and shut the door, leaving the landlord on the steps. I'd only gotten home from Atlanta the night before everything happened, and I'd been awake pretty much since then and I was tired then and I was still tired and Molly was off smoking crack and turning tricks and doing whatever determined crazy women did.

"She didn't take much clothing with her, did she?" Mrs. Borgan asked.

"No." I knew what she was getting at but I suddenly didn't care. "No, she only took a few things."

"Hmm." Mrs. Borgan sat the fern and the skull down and wandered off towards the bedroom.

"Microwave roasted chicken," Sullivan said. "How

can it get brown and crispy in a microwave?"

"Fuck if I know," I said.

"Yeah," Sullivan said. After a moment he said, "I like my chicken skin crispy."

We sat there in the hot dim room. I could hear the old lady moving stuff around in the bedroom.

"Have you ever taken a personality test?" Sullivan asked.

"No," I said. I looked at him. Squinted, even though we were inside. "What?"

"A personality test," Sullivan said. He reached over and got another can of beer out of the cooler and opened it. "They have these tests where they figure out what your personality style is." He took a long drink of beer. "We use those at work so we can work better as a team."

"I'm not on a team."

"Me," Sullivan said, "I'm an extrovert. I figure you for an introvert. I don't know about Molly, though—I never could figure her out. But I bet if you guys took one of those tests you could figure out how your personalities all fit together."

"Yeah, but right now I'm not real interested in how our personalities fit together."

"That's because you're in mourning," Sullivan said, nodding. "You're experiencing deep grief. That's to be expected at this stage."

Mrs. Borgan came out of the bedroom with an armload of Molly's clothes—blouses, shorts, a couple of her nice work suits.

"These all need to be laundered," she said. "They all sort of smell like dog stuff. You know? I told Molly I'd look after her things if something happened to her." She headed for the door.

"Don't forget your skull," I said.

"I'll be back!" she called from the porch.

"I've got some books you should read," Sullivan said. "They're all about relationships."

"I'm not in a relationship," I said. I stared at the blank TV. There was a big spot of light reflected from the open door.

Then the spot of light went dim and there was a knock on the door frame. I looked up and Alma Garcia was there. She lived next door to old Mrs. Borgan, and her husband worked for the same federal agency I did. She smiled and waved at me through the screen and came on in.

"I heard you guys are having a sale."

"Not really."

Alma looked around. "Wow, it really is bad in here, huh?"

"Oh, you should've seen it before," Sullivan said. "Dan's really been working on getting things straightened up."

I guess he was trying to help me out, make it seem like I was taking control or whatever.

"I heard you left Molly and she went crazy," Alma said. "Billy says he hasn't seen you at work for a while."

"Well, they sent me off to Atlanta to work on the task force for six weeks," I said. "I've been gone."

"Ah," she said, as if that explained everything. "I'm glad Billy doesn't have to travel. I might go crazy, too."

"Care for a beer?" I asked.

"Thanks," Alma said. She got a beer from the cooler. "It's awful hot in here."

"His electric's off," Sullivan said.

"I thought it was kind of weird you guys didn't have the game on," Alma said. "Billy's at home watching the game." She wandered off into the bedroom.

"Want to go over to Billy's house?" Sullivan asked. "We could take the beer."

"I'm not in the mood," I said.

Sullivan nodded. "I understand."

Three middle-aged women came up the steps and into the house without knocking. They stood frowning at me and Sullivan and the living room.

"Is this the sale?" the tallest woman asked.

"No," I said.

"I saw someone leaving with stuff," she said. "We thought there's supposed to be a sale here."

"They have some nice things," another woman said. "I wouldn't want that carpet, though."

"Huh-uh."

"Look at that sofa!"

The three women went on into the kitchen.

"I'm getting tired of this," I said. I got out of the recliner and went out on the steps and sat down. It was a little bit cooler outside, actually, though brighter. I had some sunglasses somewhere, though I didn't remember where. In the car, maybe. Probably. Sullivan came out a moment or so later, carrying the cooler. He placed it on the grass in front of me and pulled out a couple of beers. He handed one to me. Then he closed the lid and sat down.

"You have to think of this as a new beginning," Sullivan said. "This is a time to grow. You're starting over."

A neighbor kid—he was from down the street, I think, I couldn't remember his name, he was just some kid— came around the corner of the house pushing my lawn mower.

"Hey!" I yelled. "Put that back."

The kid looked at me and blinked, wide-eyed and innocent. "Mom said I should get this before someone else did," he said.

I thought for a minute. Despite the dry summer, the grass was long and needed cutting.

"Okay," I said, "you can have the mower if you cut the grass first."

"That's the idea," Sullivan said. "You have to teach kids values."

The kid frowned at me, then shrugged and began pulling at the starter cord. The engine caught and the kid began pushing it quickly across the yard.

Two cars pulled up in front of the house and several

women got out. They crossed the lawn and walked past me, up the steps and into the house. Alma Garcia came out of the house carrying a big bunch of things—some of Molly's clothes, one of my suits, a clock radio, and my shotgun.

"How much for all this?" she asked.

"The shotgun's not for sale," I said. The gun was in its vinyl case, and she was holding the case by the handle. I took it from her and handed it to Sullivan. "Here, you can have this."

"Really?" he asked.

"How come he gets the shotgun?" Alma asked.

"He's been helping," I said.

Alma saw the justice in that. "Well, how much for everything else?"

I shrugged. "Ten bucks."

"Oh, come on," she said. "I'll have to wash everything. How about eight?"

I shrugged again. "Whatever."

Alma slung my suit over her shoulder, struggling with all of Molly's clothes, and pulled some money from her jeans pocket. She was off balance and couldn't see what she had in her hand.

She said, "Here."

I took the money and counted it. "That's nine," I said. I reached up and stuck the extra dollar back in her hand.

"Thanks," Alma said. She started down the steps. "I'll be back!" she said over her shoulder.

Sullivan pulled the shotgun out of the case and looked it over, nodding.

"It's not that valuable a gun," I said. "I just saw it at a pawn shop one day and sort of bought it on impulse. It shoots good, though."

Sullivan placed the shotgun across his knees. "I really appreciate this," he said. He reached over and touched me on the arm. "You know, I think you're going to come through all this just fine."

I shrugged, suddenly embarrassed. The kid pushed the lawnmower by us and sprayed the two of us with grass clippings. I covered my beer to keep grass out of it.

I said, "You know, she could have at least fed the dogs—or boarded them when she left."

"I know it," Sullivan said.

"And she could have paid the electric bill."

Sullivan said, "Yep."

Goddamn Molly.

A woman I had never seen before came out of the house carrying a big rattling box.

"How much?" she asked.

I said, "Let me see."

She set the box on the porch next to me and I looked over into it. Kitchen stuff, mostly—toaster, blender, coffee pot, a few plates and cups. But the deer skull was sitting on top.

"The deer skull's spoke for," I said. "Ten bucks for everything else."

"Spoke for?"

I took the skull and set it aside.

"I was gonna give that to my little boy. He likes stuff like that." The woman opened her billfold and pulled out a ten. "You know, you could make this a lot easier for everyone if you had everything marked."

"Okay," I said. "Next time I will." I stuck the bill in my shirt pocket.

"Have a nice day," the woman said. She went down the steps and across the lawn carrying her box.

Sullivan stood up and leaned the shotgun against the house. He pulled two more beers from the cooler and closed the lid and sat back down. He handed me one of the beers. I hadn't yet opened the last one or finished the one before that.

"Thanks," I said.

I looked away from him, watching the woman carrying the box down the street. A car was pulling up in front of my house with a couple of women in it. Oh, what the hell.

"Well—" I said, and stopped.

The kid with the lawnmower made another pass by us, gave us another shower of dirt and dried grass. The women in the car were getting out. One of them was looking at me.

"Well," I said. "What the hell. You might as well take the air conditioner, too."

The Endless Inning

I took a couple of pills before I left the house to play softball—Dilaudid, a synthetic heroin—and by the time I got to the field they were kicking in. Okay. Nice, right? It was a warm fall evening, muggy but not too hot, and I sat very still—sedated, Didlaudided—and from my seat in the aluminum bleachers I could look out to the east and south and watch big jets coming in to land at the airport, strobes flashing in the clear fall air. Miracles. The way those things could stay up. On the field in front of me, two teams from our league were playing, and though neither of them were very good, both had stomped us in earlier games. I was more interested in the jets.

After a while I saw Ana's car pull into the parking lot and come to a stop, and she got out and began walking toward me, carrying her glove. When she got close I tossed a ball at her and she flinched in surprise but managed to catch it. She climbed up the bleachers and sat next to me.

Ana asked, "Where is everybody?"

"We're it," I said.

"Maybe we should just forfeit this one and get drunk now instead of later." Ana was a trim, slim woman with sharp features. She wore tight nylon cycle shorts, black with a lime green stripe up the thigh. Yeah, I was looking at her thigh. For a while. She said, "We're gonna lose, no matter what."

I said, "True."

Past Ana, I saw Silvia's car came into the lot. She got out, followed by her little boy. His name was Willie, after Willie Mays. Her littlest boy was named Harmon, after Harmon Killebrew, Silvia liked old baseball. She climbed up and sat with me and Ana while Willie scraped around in the dirt.

Silvia asked, "How are you, John?"

"Oh, I'm in fine shape."

"Oh, I can tell," Silvia said. She reached into my cooler and pulled out a beer and opened it. She nudged Ana.

"Yeah, whatever," I said. "On our team it pays to play loaded."

The three of us climbed down from the bleachers and began playing catch behind the dugout. I threw the ball to Ana, who threw it to Silvia, who sent it back to me. Silvia was slow but she had a strong arm. Ana was quick. I was—slow, too. But still we built up a nice rhythm. My reactions were a tad hazy but I was smooth. I felt good. Ana to Silvia to me to Ana. Nice.

After a few minutes, Ana asked, "Are you guys warm yet?"

"Hell, we're hot," I said. "I need a beer and a nap."

I tossed the ball to Ana and headed for the bleachers, and I opened another beer and sat down. No time for a nap, though. One of my employees, Peg, came over. An older, gray-haired lady was with her.

"Hey, John," Peg said. "This is my mom."

"Hi there," I said to Peg's Mom. "Your daughter's a fucking hero! You know that? Our unit would be a—a—a disaster without her."

Peg's Mom looked from me to Peg and back again. She smiled crookedly at me and took a step back. I suppose she thought I was messed up.

Well, I was.

"He's like that," Peg said. "He's our shortstop, too."

"Yeah?" Peg's Mom asked. "You don't look like a shortstop. How come you're not out in the outfield?"

"I can't catch fly balls," I said.

"That's true," Silvia said. "We were at practice the other day, and I threw a ball way high to John. And he was watching this bird, and the ball came down and almost hit him in the face."

"Hit him in the shoulder," Ana said.

"It should have hit him in the face," Silvia said. "Ha!"

"It still hurt," I said. Even with painkillers.

"He has a problem with airplanes, too," Ana said.

"Airplanes!" I said. "Don't fucking remind me."

Peg's mom was staring at me. Staring. Horrified? Maybe. Disbelieving, for sure. She said, "That doesn't make any sense."

I don't think she liked me. Too bad. I probably wouldn't have liked her, either, if I'd thought about it at all.

"Yeah, it doesn't," Ana said. "We were playing a game in North Austin last week and these jets were going over all the time. And some guy popped up and John lost the ball because he was watching planes."

"What the hell," I said. "I was wondering why they don't fall out of the sky."

Silvia pointed at the planes circling off to the east. "We should call the airport and tell them to shut down for a couple hours."

"It might help," I said.

Steven and Hassan and Caroline drove up at almost the same time. They got out of their cars and began warming up behind the dugout. Peg went over to join them. Little Willie climbed up and sat next to Silvia. Keith came and sat down with us, looking glum. He took one of my beers. It was only about five minutes until the game was supposed to start. The stands were starting to fill with people from work—we usually had 30 or so people at our games, witness to our futile helplessness.

Peg and Hassan came back and sat down. Hassan smelled like a barroom, like gin.

"So, what've you been doing?" I asked.

Hassan pulled a beer out my cooler. "Me and Carlos stopped off and had a couple drinks on the way here."

"Oh? Carlos is coming, is he?"

He popped the beer open and took a long drink. "Man, you know him, he's always late."

"Shit, man, you're always late, and you're here."

"Here they come," Silvia said.

Carlos and his sister, Theresa, came walking around the backstop. Carlos carried a bat bag and a poster and looked excited. Theresa wore short shorts and you could see the bottoms of her but bouncing around.

"Everybody here?" Carlos asked.

"We've been waiting for you," Silvia said.

"I'm here now." Carlos reeked of gin, too. I was sort of jealous.

Peg looked at Theresa. "Are you pitching again?

Theresa blinked. She was stoned. She asked, "— what?"

Peg asked—slowly, "Are...you...pitching...again?"

"Uh—I think so," Theresa said.

"Aw, shit," Peg said. She was our catcher. "We're gonna lose for sure."

Theresa looked at Carlos. "I'm getting better, huh?"

"I doubt it," Peg said. "We better get you warmed up, though. C'mon." Peg picked up her glove and a ball and took Theresa over by the dugout.

"I just want to win one game this season," Ana said.

"Too bad," I said. "Theresa's still pitching."

"Hey," Carlos said. "She's our secret weapon, you know? All the guys on the other team will be looking at her, not the ball. They'll all strike out."

"They'll all be looking at her, and they won't have

to take their bats off their shoulders," I said. "Theresa will walk 'em. Shit, man, she walked in twelve runs last week!"

"I've been working with her," Carlos said. "She's getting better. And she's relaxed tonight—she's not nervous."

"Let's hope."

The first game ended and the other teams came off the field. They gathered their gear and emptied the dugouts. It was our time. I picked up my bat and glove and stood up.

"Now I'm nervous," Silvia said.

"Oh yeah?" Hassan asked. "You afraid we're gonna win, or something?"

We stashed our gear in the dugout. I hung my bat on the bat hook. We were the home team this week, so we batted last. Of course, we might never get to bat at all. Carlos hung our poster at the end of the dugout and went out to give his lineup card to the umpire. We all gathered around to look at the poster. Carlos worked in the graphics shop at work, and he had made a fine poster, with our team's name—Oh No! Not Again!—at the top, and a nice diamond with our names on it showing our positions: Carlos and Keith in right field, Hassan and Caroline in left, Steven at first, Ana at second, me at short, Silvia at third, Peg catching. Theresa was the pitcher. We may have been a crummy team, but we had the best poster in the league. Ana and I took our gloves and went out onto the field. Steven and Silvia followed us. Theresa and Peg were already warming up.

"Oh no!" I said. "Not again!"

Ana was scuffing in the dirt around second base. She let out a yell—a scream—and looked at me and grinned. Steven began throwing balls to us: infield practice. I picked a grounder out of the dirt that he threw me and fired the ball back at him as hard as I could. Steven flinched and ducked and the ball sailed over his head and crashed against the fence behind him. Ana looked at me and laughed. I'd never seen a guy as afraid of the ball as Steven—no one had. He flinched every time a ball came his way.

"Be careful there, Steven," Silvia called to him. Steven recovered the ball and threw it to her, bouncing the ball through the dirt. Silvia fielded it and threw it to me. I stepped on second base and threw it softly back to Steven. He flinched as the ball entered his glove and dropped it.

"That would've been a double play if you hadn't of dropped the ball," I said.

"Have we ever made a double play?" Ana asked.

"Will we ever make one?" I asked.

Everybody was on the field. The first batter was at the plate, taking practice swings.

The umpire called. "Let's play ball!"

"Oh, shit," Ana said. "I hope this is quick."

The batter stepped up to the plate, and Theresa walked him on four pitches. In co-rec ball, if you walk a male batter, the next female batter takes a base, too. So now we had two runners on. Theresa walked the next batter, a man. Two more runners got on base, and the first batter walked in. We were down one to nothing.

"All right!" Silvia yelled. "We still got a no-hitter going!"

The next batter came up, a great big fat lug of a guy. I'd seen him play before.

"Get back!" I called to Hassan and Caroline in left field.

"We're back!" Hassan yelled to me.

"Way back! Get back further!"

Theresa pitched to the big lug. It was a ball—way outside—but the big lug swung at it and connected with the end of his bat. There was a big ringing clung and the ball was screaming overhead into left field. It went in a nice ballistic arc and came down about thirty feet behind Hassan. Hassan turned to run after it but he wasn't wearing cleats and he slipped and fell down. Then

Caroline was down, too, and both the left fielders were rolling in the grass, and the ball was rolling, rolling all the way to the fence, and Carlos was racing over from right center to get it. I ran out into left field to be the cutoff man. But when Carlos got the ball he ignored me and fired the ball back into the infield, where it bounced past Theresa and rolled to the backstop. Peg didn't even bother trying to catch it. The big lug was a fast big lug, and had already scored. We were down five to nothing.

"At least he cleared the bases," Ana said. "We don't have to worry about anybody scoring for a couple minutes."

Theresa walked the next two batters, and the bases were loaded again—women at first and third, a man at second. The next batter swung at the first pitch and missed.

"Strike!"

"Way to go, Theresa!" Silvia yelled.

The batter connected with the next ball and he hit a grounder to Ana. Ana stopped it but had trouble picking it up. The woman at first was fast and had long legs. She came charging down the base path at me. Finally Ana got the ball to me and I tagged the runner, but she beat me to the bag by just a bit. I held the glove against her butt as she teetered on the bag.

"She's out," I said.

"Safe," the umpire said.

"You sure?"

"Yep," the umpire nodded, and I took my glove off the woman's butt and tossed the ball back to Theresa.

Ana came over to me and whispered, "You tag her good enough?"

"I'll tag you one of these days."

She rolled her eyes. "I can hardly wait."

Theresa walked the next batter, a woman. A run scored. Then she walked the next batter, a man, and two runs scored. Eight to nothing. The next batter, a man, hit a grounder to me. Ana wasn't in position to cover second and force the out so I threw the ball—softly, with reservations—to Steven, at first. He flinched and the ball bounced past him and into the dugout. The runners were all speeding around the bases. Steven scrambled after the ball, got it, and threw it to Silvia, at third. The runners were going. It was a long throw and Steven's arm wasn't the best in the world, and the ball bounced in the dirt and past Silvia to the fence. All the runners scored.

Twelve to nothing.

In the bleachers, our friends from work were all drinking beer and wine coolers and yelling. I could see my boss pointing at something and laughing. Probably at me. At us, for sure.

The next batter was a woman. She took the first two pitches, balls, and swung at the third. She hit the ball weakly to Ana, who pulled it out of the dirt—nice move—and tossed it softly, underhanded, to Steven.

Out!

"One down!" I called. "Nobody on!"

"We got 'em where we want 'em!" Silvia yelled.

The Big Lug was at bat again. I looked to left field and this time Hassan and Caroline were deep. Theresa pitched another bad pitch, but the Big Lug swung at it and hit it, not as hard as before but the ball went sailing over my head and out into left field. It dropped well short of where Hassan and Caroline were positioned. They ran forward toward the ball. I ran out into the field. Hassan slipped and fell again but Caroline was on the ball and she had it. I held up my glove for the cutoff but Caroline threw past me to Silvia. The Big Lug coasted into second.

"Hey, man, you ought to fucking hit it to the same place every time," I said to him. "You're confusing the outfielders."

"Tough." He was puffing, out of breath.

Theresa walked the next batter, a woman. A man came up to bat. He swung at the first pitch and fouled it off. He hit the next one, hard, and the aluminum bat rang. It was a line drive, coming straight at me. The ball seemed to have a yellow tint under the lights and I could see it spinning as it came.

I was slow—slowed.

Dilaudided.

Bam!

The ball hit me in the chest before I could get my glove up for it, it hit right square over my heart, and it bounced straight up, hitting the bill of my cap—knocking my cap off— and going on up, on up. And the ball disappeared.

The ball was—gone—

I looked around. The Big Lug was running.

I didn't hurt—then.

I asked, "Where the fuck's the ball?"

"Behind you!" Ana yelled. She was running toward me.

I turned around and saw the ball slowly rolling into left field. I grabbed it and looked up. There was no play at first and Ana was away from second, on my side of the bag. The Big Lug was going home. Peg stood in front of the plate with her glove raised. I fired the ball at her, willing the ball from my hand to her glove, and Peg—good, solid Peg—Peg with the mom who didn't approve of me—had it and was reaching down for the tag. The Big Lug was trying to slide under her, raising dust, and they collided and there was more dust and Peg got knocked down and our drunken coworkers were all screaming.

Peg held onto the ball.

"Out!" the home plate umpire yelled.

Peg rolled off the Big Lug and tossed the ball back to Theresa.

"Nice play," the second base umpire said.

"Peg!" Ana yelled. "Peg! Peg! Peg!"

Silvia came over to me.

I had my hand over my chest. Now I was hurting. Dilaudid's supposed to be a painkiller, but, yeah, it hurt.

"You okay?" Silvia asked.

"I think I'm having a heart attack," I said.

"Oh, that's too bad," Silvia said.

I read somewhere about some guy who got hit in the chest with a line drive, and it stopped his heart. And he died. Maybe that was happening to me.

Maybe the last thing I'd ever see was the infield dirt.

Maybe now I'd never nail Ana.

I said, "I think I'm dying."

"You can't die," Silvia said. "Nobody else wants to play short."

I took a deep breath. What the hell. I probably wasn't dying. And I'd probably never nail Ana anyway.

"Two outs now!" Carlos yelled from right field. "Let's sit these fuckers down!"

Silvia wandered back to her base. Theresa walked the next batter, a woman, and the next, a man. A run scored. Thirteen to nothing. Bases were loaded. The next batter, a man, ripped the ball down the first base line. Steven didn't even try to field it, he just jumped out of the way. The runners were running. Keith charged the ball but missed it and Carlos had to come over to back him up. Ana went out for the cutoff but none of our outfielders would ever hit the cutoff—ever—and Carlos heaved the ball back to the field, to Peg, and she was able to hold the batter at third base. A triple. Three runs had scored. Sixteen to nothing.

Carlos walked in from right center. I followed him up to the pitchers' mound. The batter, a woman, was at the plate taking practice swings.

"What do you want me to do?" Theresa asked.

"Get that bitch out," Carlos said.

Theresa was frowning, lower lip puffed out, her pretty face sad. She felt bad, I guess.

"We need to stop this," I said. "We get behind by seventeen runs, the game's over."

"We'll still get an at-bat," Carlos said.

"Yeah, one-two-three we're down, and that's it."

Carlos thought for a moment. He said, "I better pitch."

"All right," I said. I said to Theresa, "You gave it a nice try, kid."

"Where do you want me to play?" she asked.

"Go out to right field," Carlos said. "Move Keith to right center. Don't try to catch any balls."

"Okay." Theresa headed for the outfield. People in the stands were hooting.

"So strike the bitch out," I said.

"Got it," Carlos nodded.

I walked back out to short.

Someone on the other team yelled, "They sent in their closer!"

"The closer!" Silvia yelled. "Carlos the closer!"

The first two pitches Carlos threw were balls.

"Oh, no!" I shouted. "Not again!"

"Oh! No! Not! Again!" Ana chanted.

The next pitch was a strike. Co-workers in the bleachers cheered. The woman swung at the next pitch and hit it—a soft dull clung and the ball was in the air over the infield, rising up into the clear night sky.

It kept going up, another little miracle, another little defiance of gravity.

Yeah.

I watched that ball go up, and like the line drive I could see it spinning, could see the stitching go round and round. But unlike the line drive, it wasn't headed at me— it was headed away.

I watched the ball.

"Look out for the plane!" Silvia called.

I raised my glove and drifted backward into shallow left field. I could hear Hassan pounding up behind me.

But the ball was mine. I could see it still spinning, reeling, coming down now—or maybe that was me.

I tried to keep my eye on the ball.

Maybe the Loneliest Human in the World

There was this girl—her name was Madeleine. I could remember that much. All night while we rolled around in bed, flesh slapping and slipping, I thought about her name—I even said it a few times. It had a nice rhythm. Madeleine, Madeleine. Maddie? Maddie. Then at one point, with the bed's headboard banging against the wall, Madeleine blurted out some guy's name—Frankie, it sounded like. Frank, Frankie. Maybe it was a girl's name. I didn't care. I pressed on into her, hoping that Madeleine had someone else—some Frankie somewhere—because I knew even then that I wanted no part of her life.

No. Really.

Then we slept. Then the alarm went off at seven-thirty. It was a Saturday morning but I'd told Madeleine I had softball practice at eight, and that everyone would be pissed if I didn't show up. A lie, of course. Practice was really on Sunday afternoons. But the alarm still rang, the clock on her phone and I crawled across her to find it and shut it off.

Madeleine was awake, under me. She said, "Whoa, that is just too loud."

She put a hand to her face like she was afraid the clock was going to hit her.

"Yeah, morning came pretty quick," I said. Thickly. My head hurt some from drinking the night before but I still kissed Madeleine on the neck, felt her smile, and ran my hand up between her legs.

"No." Madeleine giggled and pulled my hand away. "Baby, it's too early."

"No," I said. "Later. Now."

"You're crazy," Madeleine said. "You're a crazy man." She kissed me, then sank back into the pillow. I was sprawled across her with my eyes closed. Tired. She smelled like sex. I guess we both smelled like sex—we'd been fucking. After a bit she said, "Move, honey, I have to go to the bathroom."

I rolled off her, onto my back. Madeleine took a couple of deep breaths, then got out of bed. She stood there looking at me—we looked at each other. The she threw a sheet across my belly and went into the bathroom and shut the door.

I tried to focus. I pulled the sheet away and sat up on the edge of the bed and looked around. My shirt and jeans were piled on the floor outside the bathroom door. Madeleine gave me a bath the night before. I guess that was nice. Socks were there, too, in the pile. Boots in the kitchen, if I remembered correctly. Okay. I stood up and pulled my underwear and jeans on, and my shirt, and I carried my socks down the hall to the kitchen. A bottle of rum was on the counter, and a bottle of warm Coca-Cola, and my boots were there on the floor next to the refrigerator. Okay. I sat on a stool and pulled on my socks and boots and stood back up. What the hell. The rum looked pretty good. I poured some into an empty glass and topped it off with warm Coke.

Madeleine called, "I'll be out in a minute!"

Okay. Whatever.

I sipped at the rum. I stepped around the little partition the separated the kitchen from the living room and looked things over. I hadn't paid much attention the night before — the only light had been over the stove in the kitchen and the living room and the hallway had been dark and shadowy— but now, with the bright morning light streaming in, the room looked lonely and cold. It was bleak. There was a huge 56-inch Sony television mounted on the wall opposite an expensive-looking couch covered with some sort of shiny, pale pink material. A chair. Some cushions. A little table in front of the couch with the TV's remote control on it. And that was all—no pictures, no magazines, no books, no CDs or DVDs—nothing personal. I stood there with the rum in my hand and really almost winced. It was just so sad—really, I've been in motel rooms with more personality, seen pages of catalogs that looked more lived-in.

"There you are."

I turned and Madeleine came down the hall and hugged me. She was wearing a fuzzy pink robe, and I ran a hand down her back, across her meaty round butt, and she stuffed her hands in the back pockets of my jeans and pulled me tight. Her hair was wet—apparently she'd jumped in the shower and back out while I got dressed. I kissed her on top of her head.

"You're drinking before practice?" she asked.

"I dunno," I said. "We drink during the games, might as well do it right."

"Mmm." Madeleine pushed away from me, and then laughed. "You buttoned your shirt up crooked, silly. Everyone will laugh at you."

"Let 'em laugh," I said, but I stood still, my arms spread, and Madeleine unbuttoned my shirt and buttoned it back straight. I just stood there and looked past her, at the room. I couldn't get over it: TV, TV remote, couch, chair, cushion, table.

Nothing else.

It was fucking desolate.

"You like my place?" Madeleine asked.

"Yeah—you've got a lot of room," I said. What the hell. "I suppose you've just been here a little while, huh?"

"Oh, no," Madeleine said. "I've been here three years. This is home."

I put an arm around her shoulder and drained the last of the rum and winced.

Three years!

Jesus.

Madeleine turned and faced the room, leaning back into my chest. I think she was smiling.

"Yeah, this is where I watch TV, this is where I eat, this is where I do everything." She turned again and looked at me, all big brown moist eyes and dripping wet hair. Her hair smelled like lavender shampoo. She asked, "You'll come over sometime, won't you? You want to watch TV with me sometime?"

"Sure." I barely got the word out.

I stood looking at the bare wall.

I couldn't even look at her.

I was just standing there.

Madeleine—Madeleine's life—this sad goddamn empty room.

I didn't ever want to see this room again—I didn't ever want to see her again, either. And even the night before I was wondering why I was fucking her. I felt silly, stupid, glad that no one I knew could see me with my ass up in the air, banging the bed against the wall. All I wanted was to get off and get going, to just get it the hell over with and get away.

And even when we were talking in the bar the night before, I didn't think she was very interesting—she was short, with a wide, chunky butt and sad brown eyes, and she had a boring job managing a burglar alarm monitoring company, and she wasn't even very funny. At one point when we were in bed she'd leaned across me to call the alarm monitor on duty to see if everything was okay. She told me she usually worked the late shift, eleven at night until eight in the morning. She liked sitting in the office all alone, watching TV—she liked watching pro wrestling when she was at work—while she waited for an alarm to go off. When we were at the bar she told me she could talk to police dispatchers all over the country and, well, I just shrugged. Who cared about talking to cops? I wasn't even interested in talking to her! Not really. Yet there wasn't much else to do at the bar—none of the regulars were around, there was no one to play pool with—so I sat and talked with her even though I thought she was kind of stupid and dull, and then it was fairly late and she asked if I would walk her to her car. I didn't mind, and it was a warm damp evening, and quiet, a few cars heading up the street, and all of a sudden, in the streetlight shadows, I did for a moment think she was kind of cute. And so I kissed her. And she kissed back, and we stood like that for a long time, necking in the parking lot, and Madeleine was a good kisser, soft and warm, and we necked leaning back against her car, breathless, until Madeleine invited me over to her place. I followed her in my car, and I was kind of drunk, a little, and excited, and when I got up the steps and into her apartment she was already filling the tub with hot water. She wanted to give me a bath. But even later when I was fucking her—and, really, especially while I was fucking her—a little voice in the back of my mind was saying, Do not get involved with this girl. Don't do it, don't do it—

"So, you have my number, right?" Madeleine asked.

I said, "Uh, no, I don't think so."

"What's yours?" Madeleine asked. "I'll call you." She broke away from me and pulled her phone out of her robe's pocket.

I stood there.

I said, "Uh...."

And then I gave her my number. She poked numbers into her phone. Why would she call me? She wasn't going to call me. I wanted to leave—right then. Hell, before then! I looked over at the lonely living room and back at Madeleine.

Madeleine said, "There."

My phone vibrated.

I pulled it out of my back pocket and squinted at the screen. Unknown number, it said. Her. Madeleine.

Unknown.

I hit the Ignore button.

"You can text me, too," she said. "If you want."

I looked at my stupid phone and realized then that I didn't know what her last name was. She probably told me, but I'd already forgotten it. Oh well.

"So, you're going to call me?" Madeleine stood there in front of me, close, with her big brown eyes.

"Absolutely!" I said. She looked at me. I was supposed to say something more. "Maybe we can get together this week. I've got to see what my schedule's going to be like."

"That'd be great," Madeleine said. She stepped forward and hugged me. "I wish you didn't have to go so soon. I was hoping we could get something to eat, you know, and read the paper, and lay around and watch TV and stuff."

"Yeah." I thought back to fucking her the night before. Jesus. No laying around and stuff. Not even watching her big TV, and I bet she at least had a good cable package and a lot of streaming services. I said, "Yeah, but I've got to get over to practice. Everybody's probably waiting for me now."

"Okay, then."

I kissed her on the cheek and stepped back, toward the door.

"I'll call you later," I said.

"Okay," Madeleine said. She went over and unlocked the door and opened it. "Maybe I can go see you guys play softball sometime, huh?"

"Yeah, that'd be great," I said.

Now I had a sudden vision of people laughing at me. No.

Madeleine smiled up at me and I kissed her again, touching her face, running my hand down her cheek and across the front of her robe.

"I'll call you later," I said again.

"Okay."

I stepped outside, and she smiled at me. She said "See you."

And she shut the door.

I felt suddenly free.

I took a deep breath and went down the wooden steps from her apartment and out onto the sidewalk. Damn. The day was already warm and the sprinkler system was on, spraying water onto the bright green grass, and I could smell the damp earth, and where the sun hit the droplets of water there was a tiny rainbow hovering over the curb.

I glanced back at the building, glad to be out, to be free, and then I crossed the parking lot to my car. I started the car, drove out of the lot, and up the street, headed back toward my apartment on the other side of town. Done, I thought. Damn. That was stupid.

Then the light changed and I drove ahead and I thought—Well, at least I got laid.

That was a good thing, right?

✳

So. Then. A week later I was going out the door to a game with my glove and my bat tucked under my arm and I had the door key in my other hand when my phone rang—it chirruped and vibrated. I locked the door and tossed my gear into the car, and then I pulled my phone out and looked at it.

Unknown caller.

The call could be anybody. Really—calls come up as unknowns all the time. And I never answer unknown calls, so I never know who they are. They're unknown.

Standing there next to my car, I did not think for a second that Madeleine would be calling me. Might be calling me.

The phone vibrated again—a little shudder. The unknown caller had left a message.

I got into the car and started it, felt cool air from the AC blow into my face. I looked at my phone, and after a second I hit the button to call voice mail.

A machine voice said I had one new message.

Then there was a beep, and then I heard a woman's voice.

"Hi, I'm calling for Keith, I think this is his number. We met, like, last week, and—"

Aw, shit, right?

It was her, of course—Madeleine.

I mean, I wouldn't be telling this story if it wasn't her.

And sitting there in the car, I could remember her name, all right. I could feel my heart drop.

Madeleine.

"—you know, I was hoping you'd call me, but then I thought maybe you, like, washed your shirt with your phone in it and it doesn't work anymore—that sounds like something you'd do."

What the fuck? How would she know what I'd do or not do? I don't even know what I'd do or wouldn't do.

"Or maybe you dropped it, or something—so, anyway, I thought I'd call you."

Madeleine took a deep breath and then let it out, a long, long sigh.

I held my breath.

"And, you know, I was thinking maybe we could get together this weekend sometime. I was going to take my nephew up to the zoo in Fort Worth—would you like to go with us? It might be fun, you know, going to the zoo."

The zoo. The fucking zoo!

"Last time we went, we saw the rhinoceros take a

poop, and he thought that was funny—I don't know why I'm telling you that, though."

I wondered, How the fuck am I going to get out of this?

Madeleine said, "I really hope you call me." He voice was whispery, and quiet. "I had a really good time last weekend. I hope, you know, we can get together again." She paused, and sighed again. "I've never called a guy like this before. I feel kind of silly."

Then she disconnected.

I stared at the phone. The machine voice told me what key to hit, seven if I wanted to save Madeleine's message or nine to delete it.

And then I hit the key for save.

Then I wondered, Why the hell did I do that?

The machine voice said the message would be saved for fourteen days.

Why the hell did I do that?

✳

Our softball team was pretty bad, but there was at least one team worse than us—at least that night, there was—and we actually won a game. Our first win of the season. And I actually played pretty damn good: a home run, a double, two RBI singles. I didn't make any errors in the field but then only one ball got hit my way. We won, 13 to 7.

Yay, us.

Everyone but me was happy.

I sat there on the aluminum bleachers after the game, as usual, drinking beer, as usual, listening to everyone talk about the game. But I couldn't get excited about it—I kept wondering if Madeleine knew where I lived. I mean, I wasn't really worried—too much—about her being a stalker, she wasn't going to track me down and stick a butcher knife in me or even key my car. But what if she just showed up and wanted to talk to me? I could see her doing that. Talking. It would be worse that getting stabbed. Jesus. That phone call—those sighs! Really, thinking about that call I could picture her in her goddamn desolate living room, holding the phone in her hand, her giant TV on mute, sighing, filling the air with little dark farts of sadness—of loneliness, of melancholy. Every time I thought of her I winced inside.

And what if I got her pregnant?

Holy shit!

I suddenly wished I'd stopped at the convenience store and picked up some condoms. But Madeleine, leaning back against her car, said she used vaginal sponges.

Vaginal sponges—I didn't know how they worked, but they sounded kind of gross.

And what if they didn't work? What if Madeleine was bugging me because she was pregnant?

Holy shit.

Of course—she didn't really want to go to the fucking zoo. Who wants to go to a zoo? With a kid, maybe, to see a rhino poop, but who'd want to go to a zoo with me?

She'd say something like, Look at all the baby zebras! Oh, and I have one on the way, too!

I looked at my watch. It was getting late, almost ten o'clock. Madeleine didn't work Fridays or Saturdays. She'd be at home, now, staring at the TV, or trying to find patterns in the plaster on her bare white walls, or something else sad and boring.

Maybe she was thinking about me. Or about our little baby fucking zebra.

I sat there, and I couldn't believe I'd ever come in contact with someone like Madeleine.

The very thought of her made my flesh creep.

I was sitting there feeling sick, and Hennen, the shortstop, came up and sat beside me and handed me a beer.

"You're supposed to be happy," Hennen said. "We

won."

"Yeah," I said.

"You're sitting here all gloomy."

"Yeah."

I sat there with Hennen and sipped at the beer and looked around at my teammates—my friends, people I worked with, people I had known for years. Madeleine said she wanted to come to one of the games, and what a disaster that would have been. "I don't have any friends," Madeleine had said at the bar. "I guess I need to make some."

She had been living in that apartment for three years and hadn't even put a damn picture on the wall—not even a cartoon on the refrigerator.

She didn't even have a fucking friend.

She didn't even have a cat.

"You hit a home run," Hennen said.

I thought, I fucked a sad crazy lonely woman.

What does that make me?

"So you should be happy," Hennen said.

"What?" I looked at him. Oh, the home run. I asked, "Was it a real home run? Didn't they make an error out there or something?"

"Carolyn!" Hennen shouted up at one of his employees who always came to the games and kept score. "Did Keith hit a home run or was it an error?"

"Oh, a home run," Carolyn said.

I didn't even turn around and look at her.

"So it's official—you hit a home run," Hennen said. "We won the game. Cheer up."

My phone vibrated. It was sitting there on the seat next to me, and it rattled against the aluminum. I looked at it. Hennen, too.

Hennen said, "You're popular."

I picked up the phone and looked at the screen—not a call, but an email. From Facebook. A friend request. It had to be Madeleine, of course, and it was.

"The fuck," I said. I deleted the email.

"Poor Keith," Carolyn said. "He looks all bummed."

After a game I'd usually hang around with everyone and drink beer, maybe go get something to eat, and then, if we all didn't go off to someone's house for a party, I'd stop off at my hangout bar on the way home for a drink and a game or two of pool. But now Madeleine might be at the bar, looking for me. She knew where I hung out—that's where we met. Drunken hookups at the bar aren't anything unusual—once I nailed Jody the barmaid on the back pool table after closing—but, really they're nothing more than that. Fun, right? And Jody was a normal, cheerful girl who not only had a kid but a cat! And she never called me up wanting to go to the fucking zoo. We just got laid, and that was fine.

So now I couldn't go to the bar, because Madeleine might be waiting for me. And if I went straight home, Madeleine might track me down there, too, somehow. I felt trapped.

So I took another beer from Hennen and sat on the bleachers with my friends. Sat there staring off mindlessly at two other teams out on the field. I didn't even know who they were, but I bet they weren't sad and lonely and crazy.

The phone vibrated again. Another fucking call! I looked at the screen.

Unknown caller.

Madeleine the unknown.

"Call that Frankie guy or something," I said. "Maybe he wants to talk to you."

Hennen asked, "What?"

The screen went blank, and the red light went back to flashing.

I looked around. Carolyn and Sylvia were sitting behind me, talking about Sylvia's husband, I think—I heard Sylvia say, "I haven't talked to him in three days." She was always mad at her husband. Hennen sat next to me, watching the game. Dan and Hassan were standing over by Dan's car listening to music—Kanye West drifting over in the night. Other people were doing normal people things—throwing balls, drinking beers. Living. I thought about my apartment—it wasn't desolate. It looked lived-in. I had a map of New Mexico on the wall, and a calendar. A photo of the USS Iowa firing its guns, and a big one of everyone at work, all my friends, people on the softball team. Everyone smiling, normal. There were a couple of postcards my sister sent me from France. A pile of magazines, a few books. A computer. A reasonably-sized television with a DVR.

I had everything except a cat, right?

Something Else Finally Happened

Over the weekend some teacher committed suicide. A guy from the English Department. He climbed to the top row of the football stadium—which is a huge stadium, it must be at least 8 or 10 stories tall—and jumped off on the street side, flying off to the west, falling, and smashing up dead on the sidewalk. Most people heard about it, some people talked about it. What it meant, why he did it. Nobody knew. My boyfriend said it would've made more sense if the guy had killed himself during football season.

Anyway, the guy died on Saturday. The big news stories were on Monday. Then on Tuesday my first class was an English class, a writing class, and right away the teacher started talking about the suicide, as if it had just happened.

"When I was here as an undergraduate," the teacher said, "people here used to jump off the tower of the main building." She took a long drink from a cup of coffee and looked out the window. "But now there's a big fence around the observation deck up there, and you can't jump off, and you're escorted up there with guards, so I guess people are looking for the next best thing."

The teacher, Charlotte Griffin, was a writer, a novelist, though of course I hadn't read any of her books. She was very pretty, small and compact with streaks of natural gray though dyed auburn hair. She was from Tennessee or North Carolina or someplace back east, and had a low, slow, strong voice and a deep accent.

"Yes, I remember when I was an undergraduate," Charlotte said slowly. "This would have been 1967 or 68 or so—no, it was 1967, I remember, about a year after the shootings—and someone jumped off the tower. I was here in this building—it may have been this very room, in fact, because we could look out the windows at the mall. And we were sitting here, and we heard a scream, and then this terrible crunching, splattering noise—I don't really know how to describe it but you hear a sound like that and you know something's wrong—and then a bunch of other people were yelling out there. We all ran to the windows and looked out, and it was a nice spring day, like this, but a little bit later in the year, because the magnolias were blooming."

She held her coffee cup in her hand and stared out the window. I was sitting to her left and followed her gaze outside. We were on the third floor and all you could see were the middle branches of a big magnolia. I wondered how big that tree had been 40 years or so ago.

"Well!" she said suddenly, cheerily, looking away from the window and down at her notes. "Okay. What we're going to do today is, we're going to write in class." She looked up and glanced around the room at everyone. "What I want you to do is, I want you to write about a time you were pulling things out of a box."

"A box?" a boy asked.

"Right, a box."

"What kind of box?"

"A box box," Charlotte said. She looked at us all like we were stupid. "The kind of box you pull things out of. A box, okay? Your life, right?" She looked around the table.

"The box is a metaphor, okay?"

And nobody asked how a box could be a metaphor. But I don't think anybody knew, either.

Charlotte said, "I want you to focus on the things you're pulling out of the box. Tell us how those things represent the story of your life."

Somebody asked, "What?"

Charlotte repeated the prompt. The box, the things, the life. Okay?

Okay. I got it the first fucking time. Sort of.

"Okay," Charlotte said. She stood up, holding her coffee cup. "I'll be back in a little bit. You all get to work, now."

She went quickly out the door and the room was silent. The people who were sitting with their backs to the window all looked at the ceiling, and the people who were facing the window all looked out at the magnolia. I only gazed out the window for a moment. I knew what I was going to write about. Only one thing important had ever happened to me that involved a box, only one thing important, only one thing I felt. Though it wasn't a metaphor, it was real. But, anyway, I opened my notebook and began to write.

My Life

I was always different from everyone else, I knew it, I could feel it, I walked the halls of my high school and could feel people staring at me because I was different, they all knew somehow. But I didn't know how they knew about me and I didn't even how I knew about me, it was just a feeling that my life had all been made up by somebody else and I didn't even have a vote, nobody asked me anything. I watched my parents closely, and my little brother, I spied on them, and nothing they did gave away the secret, if there was a secret. I was just different, that's all. But I kept on being a spy, I had to find out why I was different. I watched my parents,

I went through their papers and pictures, and I finally found out the truth. I found my birth certificate! It was at the bottom of a deep box under a bunch of my baby things, in a packet with some other legal papers, I looked at my birth certificate and at my parent's marriage license, and found that I had been born only four months after my parents were married! I couldn't believe it! I couldn't believe the lie they told me, the lie they told everyone, the lie they lived. I ran downstairs and showed it to my mother and she started to cry, she said it happened while they were watching tv and it didn't mean she loved me any less than my brother, she said it didn't matter, but I know it did. I finally knew why I was different than everybody else, I finally knew why people

Charlotte came back into the room then, carrying another steaming full cup of coffee. She slid into her chair, careful not to spill anything, and set the cup down and looked at her watch.

"Is everybody ready?" she asked. No one said anything, but a couple of people nodded. A few people were still scribbling away. I was watching everybody else. Charlotte said, "Okay, why don't you pass all the papers up to me, and we'll go through them."

I pulled my story from the notebook and handed it to Charlotte—I was sitting right next to her. People began passing their papers up each side of the long table, talking to each other, laughing nervously. I thought of something and looked at Charlotte.

"You're not going to read these out loud, are you?"

"That's the idea," she said. She was stacking the stories in a neat pile.

"I didn't know this stuff was going to get read out loud." Other writing classes I'd had, the students would read and not the teacher, and people could choose if they want to read or not. They had a choice.

Right now, I'd choose—not.

Charlotte glanced at me and arched an eyebrow. "It's on the syllabus. On Tuesdays we write in class and discuss our writing."

I opened my mouth to say something but didn't. I'd looked over the syllabus, of course—I'm not that bad of a student. But discussing something is not reading something out loud—and it's really not having the teacher read something out loud. I thought this would be different. I didn't want her to read my story to everyone. Actually, I didn't really even want Charlotte to read it by herself, alone.

I suddenly wondered why I'd written it.

"Do you want to read it out loud?" Charlotte asked me.

"No!" I glanced around the room, horrified. I'm sure I looked horrified, too, but Charlotte wasn't paying attention to me.

"Do I have everybody's story?" Charlotte asked the class, loudly. She looked around the table and people nodded. "Great." She looked at the pile of papers. "The first one is Trey's." She looked up at Trey, a tall blond guy sitting at the far end of the table.

"Is that okay?" she asked. "Someone's got to be first."

Trey shrugged and looked embarrassed.

"Great," Charlotte said again. She began reading out loud. It was some story about playing basketball in the state tournament. Actually, it wasn't about playing basketball at all, it was about taking the bus to the state capital to play in the state tournament, and then taking equipment out of a box. I didn't get it.

"This is very fine," Charlotte said. "I like it. I could see a novel starting off like this. You've written things before, haven't you?"

Blond Trey blushed and nodded.

The next story was by a snooty girl named Hillary. It was something about getting kicked out of a private school because of some drug thing, and having to go to a public school, and how she was worried about people gossiping about her. Big deal. So what. Who cared.

"Well, this is okay," Charlotte said. "But only just okay. You kind of get away from the main narrative point there, don't you think?"

Hillary nodded. "I didn't know what to write."

"And where's the box?" Charlotte asked.

Hillary shrugged. The stupid snob. She didn't even write the prompt.

"It'll come," Charlotte said. "Don't worry."

My story was number three. I could see it on top of the pile of papers. I could already feel my face turning red. Don't read it, I thought. We're out of time. Class is over.

Please.

"What I'm trying to do," Charlotte said, looking around the room, "is to get you all looking at events as narrative. Something happens, then something else happens, then something else happens—and because of those three things, something bigger else happens. You see? In Hillary's piece too much stuff gets thrown together at once, while Trey's piece is more orderly and gradual. It builds. You see what I'm talking about?"

A few people nodded. Most people just stared blankly at her. I just stared blankly at her.

"I don't know if any of you have read Karl von Clausewitz, the Prussian military philosopher? Have you?" No one said anything, though a few people jotted down the name in their notebooks. Showoffs. "A lot of the elements of warfare he observed and wrote about in the Napoleonic Wars are applicable to fiction. They work in writing just as well as in war. One of the important things Clausewitz said was that decisions made in war—or, I say, in writing—have results that are entirely and completely unforeseen when the decision is made. When the something else finally happens, the somethings that preceded it will have not necessarily predicted it, you know? The else is a natural and organic outcome of the preceding events. You understand?"

By now everyone was staring at her with totally blank expressions on their faces. Charlotte stared back at us for a moment, and then she gave a little sigh and picked up my paper.

"Okay," Charlotte said, "Amber's story is next. She even has a title. It's called 'My Life.' Very original."

She began reading out loud in her low, harsh, hillbilly voice. I couldn't stand it. Every word pierced me. Every sentence was like a wooden stake being driven into my heart. I've seen the old black and white vampire movies and I know all about wooden stakes and that's how I felt—like the stake was in my heart, like my flesh was rotting and curling away, my guts boiling off in a mist, my skeleton exposed in a black box. She kept on reading until there wasn't anything left of me but a skeleton in a box. There just wasn't. I just looked down at the table.

Then she stopped reading and I glanced up a little.

"Well," Charlotte said, "this won't do." She was looking at me. "It's not even really a story, you know? I mean, it could be a story, but it's not. It's an anecdote—it's just a bunch of stuff happening. And the subject matter is really pretty banal, isn't it?" Charlotte looked around the class. "I mean, doesn't everyone in high school feel different from everyone else?" A few people nodded. Hillary the bitch nodded. Charlotte frowned.

I thought of my mother on that day I had confronted her. How she cried. She told me about the show they'd been watching: Wheel of Fortune, the stupid game show. It came on after the local news, and my Mom's parents weren't home. I couldn't get her to tell me the words the contestants were trying to spell—I knew she remembered, of course she did—how could she forget?—but she wouldn't say anything about it. I think about that a lot. Wheel of Fortune is still on, and I still watch it every time I can, and nobody else knows why.

Charlotte looked at my paper for a moment longer and then shrugged and frowned and put it face down on the table. That was that, I guess. I was old business. Over. A skeleton. Charlotte pulled another story from the pile.

"Okay, our next piece is from Kaitlyn. It doesn't have a title. Is the lack of a title deliberate?"

Kaitlyn shrugged.

My focus on the class evaporated, just like my flesh and blood and guts. Now there really wasn't anything left of me. I wanted to get up and run from the room, but I didn't want to draw attention to myself—I guess that's an indication that there really was something left, some sort of pride, something left to be destroyed—but at the time I just felt empty and alone and horribly, horribly naked.

Charlotte kept on reading. I didn't listen. I sat with my head down, waiting for the bell to ring. When it did ring finally, compassionate and gentle, my savior, I stacked my books and bolted from the room. Other classes were getting out, too, of course, and I was lost in a mob of students heading for the stairwell. We went through the big old glass doors—I thought of Charlotte going through the doors years ago, going through them today—and down the worn cupped steps. Then I thought—I have to talk to her. I had to say something—tell Charlotte about the story, about my life, and what it meant. I turned and forced my way back up the stairs, against the tide of kids heading down. I went back through the old doors and stood outside our classroom. Charlotte was still in the room, talking to some people, laughing at something—me, maybe—and there were some kids from the next class milling around out in the hall, looking me over, wondering why I was standing there.

Trey came out of the classroom carrying his books. He glanced at me and stopped. I don't know, I must have looked pretty bad or something, because he looked concerned.

"Are you okay?" he asked.

"I didn't know she was going to read the stories out loud," I said.

"Oh." He looked at me and I wondered what he was thinking. Now he knew things about me. Or thought he did. He said, "It'll be okay."

I shook my head and sniffed. I guess I was crying. I kept looking at Charlotte. Trey backed away, then turned and went through the doors and down the stairs.

Charlotte came out of the room with the girl named Kaitlyn. They were talking about something and smiling. Charlotte took a look at me and stopped.

"Honey, are you okay?" she asked. Her bitter hillbilly voice—all those long diphthongs and solid hard Rs—sounded suddenly sweet.

"I need to talk to you," I said thickly.

"Okay—"

"Bye!" Kaitlyn said from behind me.

Charlotte looked up and nodded and smiled and looked back at me. She had deep brown eyes and they looked warm and soft and kind. I remembered that she had kids—she was somebody's mom.

"Is this about your story?"

"Uh-huh," I sniffed.

"Listen," Charlotte said, "this world's not built for sensitive people. Okay? You can't get all emotional all the time just because someone doesn't like what you've written."

"Yeah, but—I just need to talk to you."

Charlotte sighed. "All right," she said, "but listen, I've got to run into the office real quick. Okay? I'll just be a minute."

"Okay." I sniffled again.

"C'mon, honey." She put her hand on my shoulder and led me across the hall. The department office was two doors down and we went in and she pushed me down into a green plastic-covered chair that was leaking some sort of awful cotton stuffing. "You just wait right here. I'll only be a minute."

Charlotte said hello to the secretary and disappeared into some other room. I sat and watched people in the office go about their work—answering phones, filing stuff. A professor came in and got coffee and went back out. The chairman of the department, an angry-looking bald man, came out of his office and threw down some papers on a table. He glared angrily at me like I'd done something wrong and went back into his office. Some girl came in and talked to the secretary, wanting to drop a class. I could hear Charlotte's voice in the other room, laughing about something. It was plain that she had forgotten about me.

I gathered up my books and left the office and went across the hall and through the big glass doors and down the worn staircase. It was empty now, and quiet. I could hear my footsteps on the marble stairs echo through the stairwell.

Outside I stood for a moment in the shade of the big magnolia tree with some students who were smoking cigarettes. I sniffled and fished around in my purse, looking for some tissue. I tried to stop crying. I realized it was sort of like Charlotte had said: something had happened, then something else, then something else—and because of all that, something else had happened. Something unforeseen. My mom and dad were watching a stupid game show in the basement of my grandparent's house. They had gotten kind of friendly. My mom slid back until she was sprawled out across the sofa in front of the television and my dad was on top of her. While they did it she kept seeing flashes of the TV over his shoulder—the big-headed blonde woman flipping letters, spelling something—something. Then my mom was pregnant, and she quit college and married my dad, and they got jobs and stuff, and had my little brother on purpose. Then I went off to college and made a fool out of myself. It was all a series of decisions with unforeseen results.

I dried my eyes as best I could and walked across the mall, squinting in the bright late winter sunshine—a skeleton, a zombie, somebody dazed and dead and rotted away. I looked up and noticed that the flags in front of the tower were at half-mast, in honor of that teacher who had committed suicide.

Corky the Squirrel

For once I had some good news, and I wanted to tell everyone—my family, that's everyone—and so I gathered them all together in the kitchen, a rare enough thing for us all to be in one room at one time, and I was about to speak, when a grey squirrel stuck its head in under the flap of the dog door.

And I paused.

Laurie, Brittany, Tyler—they were waiting, impatiently, I guess, for me to say something, but I was looking at the squirrel. It seemed healthy, sleek and fat, and it nervously regarded the back of Brittany's calves before it came into the room and sneaked over to the food dish of our golden retriever, Brick. The squirrel picked up a piece of dry food and began gnawing at it furiously.

"Where's Brick?" I asked.

"You want Brick here, too?" Brittany asked.

I lifted my head, pointing with my chin to the squirrel. Everyone turned and looked, and the squirrel—somehow aware of the attention it was receiving—stopped chewing and looked around. Looked at me. It still held the dog food in its paws and its little black eyes were shining.

"Oh, that's just Corky," Laurie said.

"Corky," I said. "We got a new pet and no one told me?"

Laurie said, "Well, he's not really a pet."

She already knew about what happened at work, she knew what I was going to say.

"He certainly seems right at home," I said.

Again, the squirrel was looking at me.

"What's the big deal about the squirrel?" Brittany asked. "He's cute."

"He's very cute," Laurie said.

I stood up, and the squeal of the chair on the tile floor—or maybe just my movement—frightened the squirrel, and it bolted for the door. But in its panic it couldn't find the flap and instead turned and headed along the wall under the kitchen table. Brittany jumped up off from her stool screaming, and Laurie grabbed her coffee and backed across the kitchen to the stove. Even Tyler, who had been sitting quietly, bored, jumped up and backed away.

"Everybody calm down," I said.

"Do something!" Brittany shrieked.

The squirrel reached the corner and turned back and headed for the door. Tyler kicked a stool at it and the squirrel took off in a leap, sailing from beneath the table halfway across the room, where it landed on the edge of the oven—right next to Laurie's knee. She screamed. Then the squirrel jumped again and darted behind the refrigerator.

Brittany ran yelling down the hall to her bedroom.

"Oh, come on," I said.

I went around and opened the door that led to the garage. Then I went over to the fridge and nudged it a little. The squirrel stuck its head out and saw the open door immediately and ran for it, scooting out past my feet—past Laurie, past Tyler—and through the door to some hiding place on the far side of Laurie's car. I went back and closed the door and sat back down at the table and looked around.

"End of crisis," I said.

Laurie took a sip of her coffee and sat her cup on the kitchen counter. She said, "I'll go find Brittany."

Tyler and I were left sitting alone at the table. "So," I asked. "How's it going?"

"Okay, I guess," Tyler said. He was at that stage teenaged boys get when they sit around all slack-jawed and silent. He stared at the floor, mouth open, and then he looked up at me. He said, "I saw that lady out there again."

That lady was Michelle Cooper, across the street. She'd had a baby, and she carried it around in a sling while she gardened, and sometimes she breast-fed it while out on their front lawn.

I said, "Yeah?"

Ty said, "It's gross."

"Don't look," I said. Back in my day, teenage boys liked boobs.

Laurie and Brittany came back into the kitchen and sat down.

"Well, I got the job," I said. "I'll be division manager for application development and enhancement."

"That's great!" Laurie said. I texted her after the meeting, of course. I think she really was happy.

"Ah," Brittany said. "So now you're going to get me a car, right?"

"No," I said. I glanced at Ty. He was staring out the front window at Michelle Cooper. I said, "You don't get a car, either."

"Huh?" Ty asked.

"He can't even drive," Brittany said.

I started to say, You can't, either—thinking of the drivers ed car at school she put in a ditch, the dent she put in my Highlander. But I didn't say that. I said, "We'll see."

"Good," Brittany said. "That means I get a car!"

Laurie said, "We'll see."

I said, "I thought we'd all go out to dinner and celebrate."

Nobody said anything.

Just then the squirrel stuck its head back in under the flap of the dog door. It peered into the room—at me.

"There's that damn squirrel again," I said.

Brittany jumped up and the frightened squirrel ducked back into the garage.

"Tyler, go close the garage door so he can't get in," Laurie said. Ty sort of sneered—he didn't even begin to stand up.

"No, that won't do any good," I said. "The squirrel's hiding under the car. Close the garage door and he'll just get trapped inside."

"If Brick would just defend his food...." Laurie said.

"Mom, Brick is old. He couldn't fight a squirrel if he had to."

"That's true," I said. I stood up and walked over to the sink and rinsed out my coffee cup and placed it in the dishwasher. "Didn't we have a rat trap around here somewhere?"

Laurie asked, "You're going to kill it?"

I nodded. "Sure."

"So why do you want to kill it?" Tyler asked. He looked up from the floor at me and squinted.

"Well, it'll only get killed if it gets caught in the trap," I said.

My family stood silently in the kitchen. I turned and squatted and opened the cabinet doors under the sink. One winter I found a rat's nest out back in our gas grill, and I had to set traps to catch them. I knew those traps were around somewhere.

I said, "We can't have wild animals coming in and eating all our food."

"That's what Hitler said, right?" Tyler asked. "The Jews were eating all the food?"

"What?" I turned and looked at Tyler. That kid.

"But it's just dog food," Laurie said. "And it's not even a wild animal. It's a city squirrel."

"Well, it's the principle of the thing." I bent back down and pushed aside the drain cleaner and disinfectants and groped around the back of the dark cabinet until I felt the splintery wood of an old-fashioned rat trap.

Brittany said, "What does principle have to do with a squirrel?"

"Hitler?" Tyler asked.

"Little things become big things," I said. I pulled out the trap and stood up. "It's a management thing—it's sort of what I was telling the Regional Director when they interviewed me for the job. You know?"

That was a joke, I thought. But neither of the kids said anything. They were watching me. Brittany had a look on her face that crossed the line between concern and disbelief. Ty just sat there with his mouth open—thinking about Hitler, I guess, when he should have been thinking about Michelle Cooper's boobs.

I opened one of the pantry doors and looked around. I found a jar of peanut butter and pulled it out.

Britt asked, "Peanut butter?"

"A traditional favorite of rats and squirrels," I said. I opened the jar and with my finger spread a gob of peanut butter over the bait trigger. Then I bent the spring trap band back and hooked it in place.

"Don't come near me with that thing," Laurie said.

"Don't worry." I gingerly picked the trap up and carried it to the door and out into the garage. I saw no sign of the squirrel under the car, but I knew he was around somewhere. I left the trap next to the right front tire and went back inside.

"That'll do it," I said.

"Can we go now?" Ty asked.

I blinked. "Sure. I just wanted everyone to know what was going on. And I thought we could go out...."

Brittany stood up. "Katie's coming to pick me up."

Tyler got up, too, and they went down the hallway to their rooms. Brittany said something to Tyler but I couldn't hear what she said. I looked at Laurie.

"They didn't seem to be very impressed."

Laurie shrugged. "What do you want them to do?"

"I don't know," I said. I shrugged and leaned back against the kitchen counter. "Maybe be happy for me."

"They are happy for you!"

"They don't even know what I do for a living." I shrugged again and without saying anything more I wandered down the hallway to our bedroom. I shut the door and started to undress. The light in the room was dim and everything was always so neatly arranged that it reminded me of a motel room. There were some photos on the dresser—of Laurie and me at our wedding, of the kids, of our parents—but, still, always, I felt a little uneasy there, half-expecting someone from housekeeping to barge in on me. The old dog, Brick, was curled up sleeping on the far side of the bed. I tossed a sock at him and he woke up, saw me, and thumped his tail against the floor.

"You're some dog," I said. "Can't even fight the squirrels, anymore, huh? Gettin' old, huh?"

Brick got up and came over to me, tail still wagging. He sat at the foot of the bed and looked up at me. Even in the dim light I could see the halo of gray hairs around his nose.

"Yeah, you're a good ol' dog," I said.

I scratched his ears, went into the bathroom and stepped into the shower. The hot water felt good, finally. That squirrel. Strange that everyone else knew about it—had even named it. Nobody told me anything. In junior high a couple of kids I knew had trapped a squirrel and killed it and taken it to biology class for dissection. This awful, terrible stench spilled out when they cut it open, and there was a flat dead glaze in its eyes. It was dead, dead. Horrible.

I felt better when I got out of the shower. I toweled off, and I heard Brittany and Laurie talking out in the hallway. Brittany was saying something about going over Katie's house. I got a pair of gym shorts out of the dresser and pulled them on and collapsed back onto the bed. Brick woke and looked over at me and thumped his tail. We had a television on the dresser, facing the bed, and I punched it on with the remote and switched channels to CNN. Some congressmen were griping about something. I turned the sound down and stared at the picture. Even with the bright television screen the room was subdued and quiet.

The door opened and Laurie came in, carrying a couple of glasses of wine.

"I thought you might want something," she said.

"Hey, thanks."

Laurie handed me one of the glasses and scooted onto the bed next to me. Brick walked around from the far side of the bed and stuck his nose up at Laurie. She scratched his ears and he sank back down. I sipped the wine and stared at the television. Some basketball player was selling shoes.

"The kids are happy for you," she said.

"Yeah?"

"They're very proud of you."

It really was nice hearing that. Even though it probably wasn't true.

"What the hell," I said. "They don't even know what I do for a living."

"You said that," Laurie said. "And it's not true."

There was a knock on the bedroom door.

"Hey, Katie's here," Brittany said from outside. "I'm taking off."

"Okay," Laurie said.

The business news guy came on the TV and gave the closing figures for the Dow—up, a little. I settled back into the pillows and took another sip of wine. Some of it ran off my chin and spilled onto my chest. Felt cold.

"Let's go to Zundanga," Laurie said. "Just us."

My favorite restaurant. I said, "That might be fun."

"Get dressed," Laurie said.

Then there was a scream from the other part of the house.

I looked at Laurie. What?

"Brittany," she said. She was up off the bed and out the door before I could roll over and even begin looking for my sneakers. She left the door open and Brick followed her out. I could hear some more excited shouting from the far end of the house. I finally found my shoes and pulled on a t-shirt and left the bedroom, carrying my glass of wine.

Tyler was standing out in the hallway.

"What's going on?" I asked.

"I don't know," he said stupidly.

We went down the hallway to the kitchen. Brittany was standing in the doorway, looking out into the garage. I could hear Brick barking. Brittany had her hands clasped to her chest. She looked back over her shoulder and saw me.

"Corky got caught in the trap," she said.

I pushed by Brittany and went down the steps into the garage. Laurie was standing by her car and I could see Brick's tail bobbing at the far end of the car.

"You got your squirrel," Laurie said.

I walked around the car. The metal band of the trap had the squirrel pinned by the hind leg, but it was trying to drag its way out of the garage. Brick was sniffing at the squirrel, and every time he lowered his nose the squirrel would jump, and every time the squirrel jumped, Brick barked. I sat my wine down on a shelf and tried grabbing Brick by the collar but he growled and snapped at me.

"No," I said firmly, and grabbed at him again. I got him this time and hauled him back to Laurie.

"Hold the dog," I said.

"Don't hurt Brick, too," Brittany said. Tyler was standing behind her, watching me.

"He's all right," I said. I walked back around the car. The squirrel—it was a female, I saw now, two rows of nipples on her belly—was still trying to drag the trap out of the garage. Her long tail twitched as she tried to move forward. It was covered with streaks of white that reminded me of Brick's snout.

"Oh, Daddy," Brittany whined.

"Don't worry," I said. "I'll put it out of its misery."

"You're just going to kill it?" Tyler looked at me sharply. His eyes were suddenly very bright and angry. Since when did he care about a squirrel? Since when did he care about anything?

"What—you want me to leave it in the trap?" I asked. What would Hitler do?

Tyler didn't say anything. I walked past him to the back of the garage. My golf bag was there, hanging from a hook. I pulled out the first club I touched—a nine iron. I looked at the head and swung it down, hard, in a tight arc.

"C'mon, gang," Laurie said. "Let's go inside and let your dad play with the squirrel."

I glanced back at her but no one moved. They were watching me. I could hear the scrape of the squirrel's nails on the concrete of the driveway as it struggled to get away.

"I can't believe he's going to kill it," Brittany said.

The nine iron was the wrong club. It was too long. I put it back and pulled out my sand wedge. It had a heavier head and a shorter handle. I swung it and it felt good.

"Listen, you guys," I said. "This has to be done."

No one answered me. I walked back outside. I could hear my family following me. The squirrel had made it off the concrete driveway and into the grass. Brittany's friend, Katie, was sitting behind the wheel of her car, parked in the street. She was looking in my direction— the squirrel's direction—but I couldn't see the expression on her face through the tinted glass of the car window. Across the street, Michelle Cooper, the neighbor, was dandling her baby at her breast. She'd interrupted her gardening to look over at our house—at me. The Westlund kids were playing in the yard across the street and down a house or two, and they were screaming about something. They sounded strangely distant, though. It seemed like the whole world was slowing down. The squirrel saw me coming and tried to get away, but with her hind leg in the trap she couldn't get very far, very fast.

The spring grass was soft and thick. I reached out with the sand wedge and hooked the squirrel back onto the concrete. The squirrel bucked and jumped when the club touched her and I jumped back too. I glanced up sheepishly at my family but they showed no reaction. The squirrel was trying very hard to get away, so I quickly braced myself and brought the sand wedge down on her as hard as I could. She must have seen it coming, though, because she tried to jump out of the way. I only hit her on the shoulder. She squeaked—a thin, awful, crying sound— and she thrashed around in the driveway. From the corner of my eye I could see that the Westlund kids had stopped their play and were looking at me. Michelle Cooper across the street was clutching her baby and looking at me. I raised the club to strike again.

"Oh, Daddy!" Brittany said.

I brought the club down, very hard, on the skull of the squirrel. She jerked once and then lay still, her long bushy tail quivering as she died. Blood was coming out of her ear, her mouth was pulled back into a weird grimace, and her incisors were long and yellow. Her tail flicked once or twice more and then was still. I nudged her with my foot and though she was limp and still I could feel the broken bones of her skull grating together.

I said, "It's all over."

I looked up and saw my family—Brittany and Tyler and Laurie—standing in the door of the garage regarding me with—what? Revulsion? Loathing? Disgust? I couldn't tell. They just stared at me. I lowered the sand wedge and took a step toward them. Laurie let go of Brick and the old dog ran over to me and capered about my legs before going to investigate the dead squirrel.

The Quiet Sport

Ten days into a 23 day vacation—an expedition, a voyage, a mission, a fishing trip—I began noticing that I felt somewhat different. I don't know, I felt—odd. I hadn't talked with anyone since I left Dallas, not said anything more than "Thank you" or "Yeah" to waitresses and convenience-store clerks along the way, and though I sometimes wondered what was happening back at work, I never called in to see what was actually going on. And my family—my ex-wife, my son—I didn't even want to think about them. As far as I knew, cared, was concerned, they had almost ceased to exist. I really felt very strange. I didn't want to talk, and I didn't talk. The silence built up, mile after mile, across the Texas Panhandle and onto the Colorado plains, and then into Wyoming, and I grew used to it, and I liked it.

Ten days: two days of silent driving—no radio, even, just the sound of the wind and the pickup's engine—two days of driving and then fishing. I fished the Tongue, the Wind, the Big Horn, the Popo Agie, and then on to the North Fork of the Shoshone, working my way west, ever higher, heading up towards Yellowstone. I hoped that standing in a cold river for hours at a time would wash away my old self, my city self—my angry self, too used to arguing with bureaucrats and administrators and clients and fools and family. At night in my tent I dropped off to sleep hoping to dream not of people but of water, and the sound of water was the only thing I wanted to hear.

The first day on the Shoshone I arrived late—I'd loitered some in Cody, buying some fishing gear I really didn't need, and then spending three hours or so wandering around the Buffalo Bill Museum— but I was still able to find a nice campsite right by the river, private and well-screened by cottonwoods. On the far side of the river a red cliff rose, high and rugged. I could hear the water—it was a loud, fast river.

I was unloading my gear from the truck when I looked up and saw a big man with a spade-shaped beard walking down toward me along the dusty road that circled through the campground. I pulled the cooler from the truck and set it in the shade, and when I looked up again, the big man was standing there looking at me.

"Hey," I said. My voice sounded loud—louder even than the river.

"Hi," The big man said. He was looking over my gear, nodding. He was wide, and balding, and his beard and hair were an orangish burnt red. He said, "I saw your license plate when you drove in. Texas, huh? That's a long way."

I leaned against the truck. I wasn't sure what to say. I hadn't talked to anyone in so long, it was weird. In Cody I'd only grunted and shrugged when the clerk at the fly shop asked me how the fishing was. It was like I had no words left.

But now I looked at the big man, and I thought for a moment. I finally said, "Yeah, it takes about three days to get up here."

"That's a long way," the big man said. "We came from Kentucky."

I nodded. I said, "That's even further."

"Yeah, it's pretty far." Then the big man pointed to the sky. "Look! There's an eagle!"

I turned and looked in the direction the guy was pointing but saw nothing but blue sky and a few white cirrus clouds high above the cliff wall.

"You missed it. It was a bald eagle. They're nice to see. They like those cliffs, they can get a nice updraft off of there."

I looked back at the big man. I kind of wished he'd go away.

I came west to get away from people, not chat with them.

"My name's Bob." The big man stuck out his hand. It was the size of a old-fashioned dictionary.

I shook his hand. I didn't want to, really, but I didn't want to be rude, either.

"Came out here to fish, huh?" Bob nodded at my rod cases in the back of the truck.

"Yeah," I said. After a moment—a second, maybe—I decided I needed to say something more. I said, "Yeah, I've done pretty good so far."

"There's that eagle again."

I turned again and this time I saw the eagle—the white head distinct, even at a distance—gliding high above the cliff-top. In a few seconds it passed from sight. I looked back and Bob was grinning. I nodded.

"Well, they say there's good fishing in this river," Bob said.

"That's what I hear," I said. I paused again, then said, "I'm surprised, though, this campground's so empty."

"Oh, it fills up every night," Bob said. "People on their way to Yellowstone. We've been here for a week and it fills up every night."

"Huh," I said. I looked up the road and could see only one camper parked at the far end of the campground. There was a slight rustle of wind through the cottonwoods, and

I could hear the sound of the river.

"Well, I'll let you finish unpacking," Bob said. "Come on by tonight and have a beer, if you want. We're parked over here." Bob pointed downstream, down the road. "We got that big RV with the blue awning. I brought my banjo, and my son's learning to play the dulcimer."

"I might just do that," I said. Sure.

"You should." Bob stuck his huge hand out again, and I shook it. "Come on by."

"Okay."

I watched Bob head down the road. I thought, Damn. A banjo-playing giant from Kentucky. Holy shit. I pulled a beer from the cooler and sat on the tailgate of the pickup, in the shade, and opened the can. Every now and then I could hear a particularly loud car or RV laboring up the highway to Yellowstone, but mostly I could just hear the river—cold water splashing over rocks, hurrying to get down out of the mountains.

✱

The day passed, and evening came. I stood on a gravel bar below the campsite and looked out at the river, and I saw no signs of trout. The river looked promising, it looked good, though a little high and heavy and off-colored, the water flowing from a shallow gravel flat where a creek entered, under a sturdy forest-service bridge, and on down past the campground in a deep run under the tall cliff. It looked trouty, but I didn't see any active trout, I didn't see trout feeding or rolling around, and I didn't see any bugs for them to feed on. A chart on the wall of the fly shop in Cody said there were good hatches of flavelinas—Gray Drakes, a species of mayfly—coming off every evening. But I looked at the water, at the heavy fast current, the chop from the rocks and snags, and I wondered how the delicate little mayflies would be able to float on the surface long enough to dry their wings and fly away. But still they did it, of course. Mayflies, dumb insects that they were, knew more about being mayflies than I'd ever know about them, and the trout knew more about being trout than I knew, too, and the guys at the fly shop in Cody knew more about fly fishing, and the guys who wrote in the magazines. Everybody pretty much knew more than I did, or do. The world is a mystery, forever. Unknowable. Anyway. I tied a small nymph, a Pheasant Tail, to the end of my leader, with a couple of split shot a foot or so above it, and began to fish.

On the fourth cast I hooked a small whitefish, a slippery cousin to a trout, and I released it. I stepped further into the current, cold water splashing up to my waist, and I tried to reach a cast across the current so that it would float gently in the quiet water near the cliff. My casts came up a little short, and I waded deeper, over my waist, and I was able to drop the fly where I wanted it and get a decent drift. I caught another whitefish, and a little rainbow trout, and I was so intent on watching the leader, looking to see the twitch that would signal a strike, that I missed the start of the flavelina hatch. It wasn't until there was a plashy rise from a fish right in front of me— probably from a whitefish—that I backed off and looked closely at the water. And the Gray Drakes were there. They weren't there in great numbers, just enough to get the fish moving. I saw another rise, the smoother rise of a trout, over in the shadows near the cliff, and another. There were a few smaller caddis flies fluttering over the water, too, but I figured that the fish would be keying on the Gray Drakes—they were bigger, and there were more of them. Sunlight caught on their wings as they rode the choppy water, glittering, the mayflies preparing to fly off to molt, mate, and die. Nice cycle. I braced myself against the current and reeled in the line and leader and removed the split shot and the nymph, tying on the fly I wanted to use to imitate the Gray Drakes, a bushy dry fly for the heavy water. My hands were shaking a little when I tied the knot. Fish were rising. I tried to say calm—listen to that water. Then I began to cast, and I built up a good rhythm quickly, punching the fly upstream and across, getting decent drifts, and on my fifth cast a decent trout rose and sucked in the fly. There—a happy thing, for me, though not for the trout, and I could feel the angry scared live weight of the fish in the heavy current, and I saw it jump, jump—and I brought the trout in, and released it. I dried the fly and began casting again, looking for my rhythm, the rhythm, finding it, finding the fish, and the sun disappeared into the mountains and the shadow of the cliff drifted across the river until everything faded to gray and I could no longer see to cast.

It all happened so fast! The fishing—the casting, the fish, the setting sun.

I made my way back to shore in the near dark, the river still rushing, and I stumbled down the bankside trail to the campsite, suddenly tired. Drained. Depleted. Suddenly the form of an old man loomed up on the shadowy trail, an old man, fat, with his hands on his hips.

"Well, how'd it go out there?" the old man asked.

It took me a second to realize he was asking about the fishing. I thought about it—about the fishing.

After a moment, I said, "Oh—good. It was real good."

✸

I felt restless when I returned to the campsite. For the first time in what seemed like a long time I felt like talking to someone. There was the fat old man in the shadows on the trail—I could maybe find him and tell him what the fishing had really been like, now that I'd had a chance to think about it a little, about the sunlight and the shadow and the mayflies and the trout, and how the river kept trying to pull me downstream out of the mountains. But I didn't know the old man, didn't even know which site he was camped at. There was also the big guy from

Kentucky, Bob. Banjo-playing Bob, from Kentucky. I could go over to Bob's RV and have a beer or two. Talking to him in the afternoon broke my ten days of silence, and maybe that was a good thing.

Or maybe not.

After all, I didn't really know Bob, either, and maybe Bob wasn't serious about the invitation.

I rummaged around in the supply chest and pulled out a bottle of sake and a tin cup. Warm sake was always good after fishing, on evenings when it was dark and chilly out and a nice fire was burning. The coals from the steak I had for dinner were still alive, still hot, and I thought about setting the cup of saké on the grill to warm up, and then thought—well, maybe Bob would like some sake.

Before I could change my mind I hopped off the tailgate of the truck and headed down the road. The road's soft dust puffed up around my boots, so different from the hard rocks of the streambed, and it was quiet in the trees—though there was still that sound of water. I barely came around the bend when I heard the sound of a banjo twanging, so I headed toward that. There was a loop at the end of the road, and in the light of a large fire I could make out a big RV and a smaller car, and a huge flickering shadow no doubt cast by the tarp Bob had mentioned. I hesitated there in the dark, in the dust. I could hear Bob's banjo—no song that I could recognize, just picking—and I thought again that maybe Bob had not been serious when he'd invited me over. But then he seemed like a friendly kind of guy, he'd just walked up in the afternoon and introduced himself. But maybe he wasn't. How was I supposed to know people? I took a couple of steps to the side, and I saw a teenage boy sitting on a log to Bob's right—his son, no doubt, the dulcimer player. I didn't even know what a dulcimer sounded like. Bob said something and the boy laughed and looked at Bob and grinned, and Bob was grinning, too. Bob grinned and tossed another chunk of wood on the fire and then poked it into place with a stick. Then a heavyset woman came out of the RV and handed Bob a beer and the boy a soda, and I heard her say, "What's so funny?" I heard Bob voice, his answer, but I couldn't make out his words. Bob had a low voice, kind of mumbly. The woman heard him, though, and she shook her head and sat down in a chair next to Bob and put her hand on his shoulder and rubbed it. She was smiling and looking at Bob. The boy said something then, and Bob nodded and plucked on the banjo and chuckled.

Damn. I took a step back, further into the shadows. There was no way I could go talk to these people. They were totally—alien—to how I lived. They looked happy. I couldn't believe it. My own son, Brady, was in an expensive private hospital in Austin drying out. Brady had a huge red and black snake tattooed on his left arm, beginning at the back of his hand and winding across his palm and around his wrist and forearm and on up. The snake's head on the back of his hand looked like a penis. He looked like he was holding a great big floppy penis in his hand. I went to the hospital and I said, Listen, if you want to go out west with me, go fishing, I can get you out of here, and Brady just sat there and rubbed his snake and laughed and said, No, he liked it in the hospital. He said it was saving his life. I didn't understand—it didn't make sense. The hospital was in a wonderfully restored old mansion shaded by big magnolia trees and it had a beautiful garden, but it was run by a bunch of dour Lutherans and just didn't seem to be the kind of place Brady would want to be. But Brady didn't even look up, he just looked at the floor and rubbed his snake and laughed and shook his head like going on a fishing trip out west was the stupidest goddamn thing he'd ever heard of. And Brady had been a boy who'd liked going fishing when he was little—had liked it as long as we caught something, of course, because if we didn't catch anything Brady would get bored and wander off into the trees or throw rocks. But I'd thought about that, about how easily Brady could get bored, and I told Brady that he didn't have to fish with me, that we could do other things, go for a hike, go whitewater rafting, do anything he wanted to do, anything. But still Brady sat there looking at the floor and rubbing his tattoo and shaking his head, no. No. I went home and called Brady's mom, my ex-wife, and I asked her what the deal was with Brady, and all she said was that if my insurance was covering rehab, and if Brady was happy, then it was okay with her.

Bob kept picking aimlessly at the banjo. Too much family fun for me. I shifted the bottle of saké in my hand and turned to leave, and then a little-sounding dog began barking. Yapping. I froze.

"Kip!" Bob yelled. "Get back here!"

"Maybe it's a bear, Dad," the boy said.

The boy sounded hopeful. He wanted to see a bear.

"I hope to God Kip has better sense than to mess with a bear," Bob said. "Get on back here!"

The little dog stopped barking and I turned my head and saw a Pomeranian pop into the firelight, jumping up at Bob's knee. Bob patted the dog on the head and sat back in his chair.

I quickly turned and made my way back up the road in the dark. When I got to camp I threw some wood on the fire and filled the tin cup with saké and sat it on the grating next to the fire. I opened a beer and sat at the picnic table and took a deep breath.

✳

In the morning I opened my eyes and looked up at the roof of the tent and felt sick. I had some vague, weird memory of doing something stupid during the night. Vaguely stupid.

I rolled to my side and pulled the pillow over my face and tried going back to sleep but it was no use. I was awake for good. I crawled out of my sleeping bag—and found myself still dressed, still even wearing my hiking boots, I'd worn them into the sleeping bag sometime in the night, tracking mud and dirt and shit everywhere. For Christ's sake. I crawled on outside and saw the saké bottle on its side in the dirt next to the fire pit, and beer cans scattered on the ground around the trash barrel. My head hurt. I had a sudden memory of staring into the fire, drunk as shit, obsessing over Brady's mom. And all that went with that. Over and over again, a big damn circle, the same scenes came around—in particular, the time on the fishing trip to Belize when she eased out of our cabin at night and fucked my fishing guide. I mean—not the guide! It was pretty funny—almost a joke, not really but almost. Not the guide. It you want to fuck somebody, fuck the goddamn cook, or the manager, or the bartender. Don't mess up my fishing! And then of course Debra refused to even talk about it, she said it was none of my business—and maybe it wouldn't have been, we were breaking up anyway, except for the fishing—and then when we got back to Dallas we found Brady in trouble at school for passing out drunk in class. Oh well! I stood there over the empty saké bottle in front of the dead fire and I shut my eyes. No. There was no use getting into that again. No use. When I opened my eyes the fat old man from the evening before was standing out in the road, looking at my messy, littered campsite, and his lips were pursed in distaste. So what. I was just glad Bob from Kentucky wasn't there to see the mess I'd made. I ignored the old man and stumbled up the dusty road to the campground toilets—sick, sick.

✳

The campground was almost full again in the evening when I finally roused myself to go fishing. I'd spent the day in my dirty tent, chewing aspirin and reading Bernard De Voto's The Course of Empire, wishing that I'd maybe followed Lewis and Clark into Montana, fishing the Missouri, the Madison, the Ruby, the Beaverhead, and then across the Great Divide into the unknown. It might be fun to have a time machine and go back and see all that. Or I could keep on driving and go see all that now. Maybe. I thought about it, read, and dozed a little. When I finally emerged from the tent, I still felt ragged and tired and depressed, and I sat on the picnic table and drank a beer and watched a big RV try to back into a small parking slot at the campsite next door—the fat old man who'd spent the night there had fortunately left. I had another beer and I pulled on my waders and vest and tied my boots. It was too early for the flavs to come out, but I wanted to run a big nymph down that deep run below the bridge, and then when the mayflies appeared I could switch over and fish dry flies.

I headed up along the path, upstream to where the bridge crossed the river. All the campsites along the river were occupied, and people were walking the trails— couples and families, mostly—and up near the big sandbar I saw another guy fishing, though he was using a spinning rig.

I clomped across the bridge in my heavy boots. The water was a bit clearer than it had been the day before, though it was still high and cold and fast, and the sound of it pouring past the bridge abutments was exciting. It was the sound of my dreams. I began to feel a bit better.

The deep channel below the bridge dropped off very suddenly—I could stand only ankle-deep in the water; another step forward and I would have been up to my shoulders or over my head. I rigged up with a heavy nymph at the end of a long leader, with extra lead shot attached to make it sink rapidly, and began casting. There were little eddies of slack water behind the nearest bridge abutment, good places for a trout to lie in ambush for a bug, and I tried to aim my cast so that the fly would tumble into the eddy and float there for a second or two—long enough to get eaten—before the heavy current put drag on the slack line and pulled the fly away. It wasn't easy. Too many of my casts were too far off the mark, but I kept trying. At one point I glanced up and saw that there were some people on the bridge watching me, a middle-aged man and woman, and a boy and girl. I watched the line drag through the run and then I looked up again. The boy was about Brady's age and size, though fairer, with long lank yellow hair and acne. I could feel the yellow-haired boy stare at me, so I put more effort into my casting. I knew I was showing off for the boy and I was kind of embarrassed about it, but I was showing off anyway.

I started getting into the rhythm of the casting—casting the big, weighted nymph was not as much fun as casting a dry fly, but it had its own rhythm to learn—flopping the whole works upstream into the fast water, over and over again, waiting for the line to twitch and signal a strike— which wasn't happening, but still—watching the water, feeling it around my knees, listening.

And then there was a huge splash about two feet in front of me—at first I thought it was a fish, and my heart really skipped a beat. Thud—thud. But then I just as quickly realized it wasn't a fish—it was a rock.

Somebody threw a goddamn rock at me.

I looked up. The family on the bridge had crossed and was disappearing into the trees. The teen-aged boy, the one with yellow hair, looked back over his shoulder with a smirk.

Oh, that son of a bitch.

"You stupid piece of shit," I said. I said it loud enough to be heard over the river but I didn't shout. "Don't try that again."

I heard the girl—the boy's sister—say, "I told you not to do that."

The boy laughed and said something to the girl, and then he looked back at me and laughed again. Then he turned away.

Little shit-head.

My line was all tangled and looped together, and when I drew it in to untangle it I saw that my hands were shaking.

The son of a bitch.

I finally untangled the line and went back to fishing. In a few minutes I caught a decent rainbow, a nice-sized fish that felt bigger in the heavy water. I netted it and slipped the hook out, and when I bent to release it I glanced up and saw the family coming back down the road—the mother, the father, the girl, the yellow-haired boy. I dropped the trout back into the water and tensed up. The yellow-haired kid was looking at me.

I picked the fly up with a roll cast and plunked it a few feet upstream. I faced where the line went into the water. I was staring at the line, but was I paying attention to the kid.

I saw the kid duck behind a tree.

"Don't," the kid's sister said.

I looked around. Mom and Dad were well out in front of the kids, almost to the other side of the bridge. They seemed to be nice enough people, to look at them, dressed in expensive outdoor clothing.

Then the rock flew past my face.

There was a big splash but I looked up at the bridge instead of down at the water. The yellow-haired kid was standing there, smiling.

"You asshole," I said, quietly. I dropped the fly rod into the water, not even caring if the river carried it away. I stepped up onto the bank.

"Tyler," the sister said. "Come on."

I walked up through the brush and onto the bridge.

"I told you not to do that again," I said.

The kid began slowly backing away. His sister moved quicker, keeping her eyes on me the whole time.

"You piece of shit," I said.

"I didn't do anything," the kid said. He was still smiling.

I lunged then at the kid and grabbed him by his shirt front. The kid yelled and slapped at me and knocked my hat off, but I grabbed him at the crotch and lifted him up, wrestling him to the top of the railing of the bridge. The kid kicked at me, but I braced up and grunted and shoved him hard, and I pushed him over the railing, and the kid yelled once more before hitting the water, and then he disappeared. I glared at the kid's sister, who was wide-eyed, shocked, backing away to the far end of the bridge. The kid bobbed to the surface a few yards downstream and yelled again and I turned to watch him. I wondered if he'd be able to drag himself out. But the river had the kid and he bobbed under again and again in the heavy current, and the cold steel-blue water carried him downstream and around the bend. The last I saw of the kid was his hand sticking up out of the water as the river carried him away. Then, for a little while, I relaxed. Everything was still and beautifully quiet.

Cassie's Shirt

My daughter, Cassie, still seemed to me a lot of the time like a little girl, but now I was glad to see that she was no more afraid of blood than I was. Less afraid, maybe, since my fear was controlled by the fact that I knew that scalp wounds bled a great deal, and Cassie, until now, had probably not known that. Her hand held a wet piece of cloth to my cheek, dabbing at the blood, and when I tried to smile at her, she looked away, her face pale and drawn. She was afraid, some, a little, but not too much. She was just right.

"I'll be okay," I said. It was a little hard for me to talk: my lips were already swollen and my nose felt like it was packed with ice. Cassie just gazed at me solemnly.

I heard some splashing and looked down the hill. The man named Walsh was coming up from the river, waving my good fly rod in the air, and he was grinning like some redneck from a reality TV show. He came on up the hill toward us, water running from his hip boots, and beyond him in the river I could still see trout rising.

"I found your rod," Walsh said. "It's a little wet but it should be okay."

"Thanks," I said, slowly. "I didn't think I busted it."

"You sure busted your nose, though," Walsh said. He leaned the rod against a tree and sat heavily next to me on the soft carpet of pine needles, looking into my face. "That was one hell of a spill you took, man. That was the damnedest thing I ever saw." Walsh had been hiking up the river to fish the upper meadow when he saw me slip and fall.

He lifted the rag at my forehead a little and blood once again ran out—gushed out, I'd almost have to say— running into my eyes, stinging, and on down my cheeks. There was blood everywhere. I squinted and blinked and I could feel Cassie's hand in mine, gripping, squeezing. I don't think Cassie quite trusted Walsh, a stranger; but even then, banged up as I was, I knew that I could have maybe drowned if Walsh hadn't run over and yanked me out of the river. I had slipped and fallen face-first onto some rocks, sprawled out and stunned for a moment, cold water gurgling over me, around me, and poor Cassie was too small to roll me over, much less pull me out.

"We need to get you to a doctor, man, you're bleeding all over the damn place," Walsh said. "You don't have a first aid kit or anything, do you?"

"Huh-uh," I said. I never carried one. I'd never needed one before—even when I'd snagged a hook into myself I always managed to get it out without bleeding too much.

"Me neither," Walsh said. He pursed his lips and looked at me. Thinking about something.

"Cut a piece of a shirt?" Cassie asked.

"I guess that'd work," Walsh said. He hesitated, seeming not especially eager to give me the shirt off his back. Which was fine, I guessed—his short didn't look too clean. My shirt of course was useless, soaked through under my unzipped rain jacket with water from the river and my own blood.

But Cassie suddenly rose to her knees and took off her rain jacket, dropping it to the needles behind her, unbuttoning the soft red and gray flannel shirt she wore beneath. She peeled off the shirt—I could see chill bumps already forming on her skinny little arms—and handed it to Walsh.

"Here," she said. She was wearing a t-shirt with a running buffalo on it that her mother and I had bought her in Cheyenne, and she sat there soberly in it, watching us, and she shivered.

"Get your jacket back on, honey," I said thickly. "You'll get all wet."

Cassie frowned and hunched back into her jacket. I looked over and Walsh had a pocket knife out and was cutting into the shirt, then ripping a long piece out of it. He wadded up the length of flannel, then peeled away the sopping crimson handkerchief I was holding to my forehead—blood running once again—and placed the flannel across it. Then he put my hand back on the new flannel.

"Hold that," he said. "You're gonna need big stitches, for sure."

Then Walsh cut one of the sleeves off the shirt, and ripped it down the middle into a long band. He helped me sit up, a little, and wrapped the band around my head and tied it in back.

"If this were a tourniquet we could tighten it on up and pop your brain out," Walsh said. "Like a pimple. Problem solved." He was smiling but Cassie just frowned at him.

I sat back, glad to have the blood out of my face, if only for a moment.

Walsh was on his knees, holding the rest of the shirt in his hands. "I don't know," he said. "I guess I'll just leave the rest of your face alone."

"Thank you," I said. I took the rest of the soft flannel from him and dabbed it gently at the blood oozing from the cut on the bridge of my swelling nose. My face only hurt when I tried to talk or when something touched it. It was tender, very tender, and I didn't want anyone—except for maybe Cassie—to mess with it. After a moment I said, "I'm thirsty."

"Yeah, you probably need something to replace that blood, huh?" Walsh reached into his vest and came out with a plastic flask. He looked at it and frowned. "Jim Beam. Probably not too good for a head injury, though, huh?"

"Here." Cassie spoke again and I looked at her holding out a green plastic bottle of 7-Up. She unscrewed the top and handed me the bottle and I took a swallow and it was warm and flat and just right. Cassie frowned at Walsh and I turned and saw him take a hit off his flask. Cassie was something of a prohibitionist, a result of anti-drug education at her school: I remember once I was sitting in the living room, drinking beer and watching football, and Cassie had marched in and asked, "You know you're drinking a drug, right?" I'd just laughed at her and hurt her feelings. Now she was mad at Walsh and he didn't even know it.

"This is a pretty good little river," Walsh said. He sat back, relaxed, looking out over the water. Fish were rising almost everywhere in the run below us. "Mostly brookies and browns, you know, nothing really big but there's a lot of 'em."

"I know," I said. I'd brought Cassie here to catch her first trout on a fly, and she'd caught several. The day had remained gray and drizzly and mayflies had been coming off all afternoon, and Cassie had had a blast with dry flies, catching lots of brookies and a few browns—nothing really big, as Walsh had said, but Cassie was happy. It was a good day until I slipped and fell.

Walsh looked at me. "Don't see many people here from out of state. Most tourists go on up to the Bighorn or someplace famous."

"Yeah," I said. I didn't particularly like being called a tourist but I thought about it and I guess that's what we were, to him: a couple of clumsy tourists. I sucked some more at the 7-Up before I went on. "We just found this place by accident," I said. Which was not exactly true: I had been here two years before, on a trip by myself, and had found it by reading topo maps. I'd had good, easy fishing then, which was why I had brought Cassie here now.

Walsh nodded and took another hit off his flask and grimaced. "Well, it's a good little river," he said after a second. He tucked the flask back in his pocket and stood up. "So what's the logistics on this? You want me to take you all the way to the hospital in Sheridan?"

The way Walsh said "all the way"—he curled his lip, sort of—made me pretty sure he didn't want to take me all the way to the hospital in Sheridan. And if he didn't want to, then I didn't want him to. He'd already pulled me out of the river and that was enough.

"We're camped back here at this first campground," I said. I waved my hand in the direction the river was flowing. "It's not very far."

"Seven miles," Cassie said.

"Something like that," I said. Cassie was probably right, though—she was a very good navigator. "We get back there, you know, my wife can get me to the hospital." Actually, I didn't know if Patsy would be back at the trailer or not. She'd said she was going to hike down to an old sawmill and make some photographs. I hoped she'd be back by the time we got there.

"You can't drive, though," Walsh said. "Right?"

I didn't know if Walsh was asking me or Cassie. Anyway, it sounded more like a statement than a question.

"I probably can," I said. At least, I thought I could. Cassie of course had never even had a driving lesson.

Walsh sniffed and rubbed his nose. His black beard stuck out and he seemed even more bearish.

"I kind of doubt that," Walsh said. He smiled at me, sort of. "So, I guess I'll drive you guys back to the campground, and we'll get your wife, and then we'll come back up here and get your truck, and then she can drive you to Sheridan. That'll work, I think. Okay?"

"Whatever," I said. I thought, This will take all night. Maybe we can get a motel room in Sheridan. What the hell. I moved to get up and Cassie and Walsh each took an elbow and helped me. I stood, wobbling a little.

"You okay?" Walsh asked.

"I think so."

"You know you're probably concussed, right?" Walsh held up two fingers—a peace sign. "How many fingers I got?"

"On your whole hand? Five."

Walsh laughed. "Yeah, you're fucked up in the head," he said. "We better get going."

Walsh ducked back into the brush. Cassie took my heavy fly vest and put it on; it was much too big for her, of course, hanging below her hips.

"Want me to carry your rod?" she asked.

"Could you, hon?" I was afraid I might lose my balance again and fall, and this time I might be unlucky enough to break it.

"Sure." Cassie looked at me for a moment, her lips pursed, and then started looking in the vest, patting the pockets. She pulled out my sunglasses, amazingly unbroken, and handed them to me. "Put these on," she said. "You look nasty."

I took the glasses from her and tried to smile. They didn't fit very well around my swollen, tender nose but I bent the frames some and they went on okay. Walsh came out of the brush with a sturdy-looking branch for me to use as a staff. I tapped it on the ground a couple of times and it seemed good enough.

"Okay," Walsh said. "Let's get going, then. I'm parked downstream from here, and up the hill."

A few feet up the hill from us there was a path leading through the woods, parallel to the river, a game or cattle trail of some sort, and we followed that, Walsh in the lead, then me, and Cassie just behind me, nudging me occasionally on the small of the back with the butt of her fly rod. It was not hard going, but my face hurt and I was a little dizzy. The dizziness worried me, and I thought that maybe I really did have a concussion of some sort. The only thing I could remember about concussions was that you got nauseous and cranky. I didn't feel like throwing up, though, or yelling at anyone. I was just dizzy and sore and tired—and wet and cold, too. The altitude was a part of that—we were at around 7500 feet, and had only been in the mountains for a couple of days. I wasn't used to the thinner air and I tried to breathe without panting. I didn't want Walsh to know I was out of shape. A cloud opened up on us and a heavy rain fell for a few moments, and I wondered then if I was going to die of hypothermia. It seemed likely but I kept trudging on, following Walsh.

Walsh was talking the whole time, of course, though at first I didn't pay attention to what he was saying. I was just sort of staring at the trail ahead of me, glancing up every now and then at his back. Walsh paused occasionally to let me catch up, grinning at me, strong white teeth in the midst of his black beard. I didn't like the grin. It made him look like he was mocking me—mocking my clumsiness, my touristness, my out-of-stateness, my out-of-breathness. My lack of fishing ability. I resented the fact that he was having to help me home.

"You guys probably spend all your time fishing for bass, right?" Walsh asked. "They're different from trout—they're a lot more aggressive, so they're easier to catch. To catch these trout, now, though, you have to use something that looks just like what they're eating."

He paused and turned and waited for me, grinning.

I gasped, "I know all that."

Walsh pointed down at a long curve in the river. "And, like, you have to look for undercut banks and stuff, because that's where the big ones hang out."

"Yeah, no kidding."

Walsh turned and headed on down the trail. He was carrying his rod pointed behind him so that it wouldn't hang up in the trees, and I had to stay about ten feet or so back to avoid the rod tip because even with the sunglasses I worried about getting jabbed in the eye. I looked back at Cassie and she was carrying her rod and mine the same way, pointed out behind her, one in each hand, and she smiled at me a little, a small smile, glad perhaps at last to be headed back to camp. I was glad, too. Back to camp and away from Walsh and on to Sheridan, I thought. Stitches and a tetanus shot and maybe some painkillers and pizza and a motel room. That all sounded pretty good.

"I really like this place," Walsh said. He stopped and waved an arm at the mountains. "I can get off work, you know, and in twenty minutes I can go out and shoot an elk or catch a trout or do whatever the fuck I want to do. Bet you guys can't do that in Dallas, huh? You guys probably just sit around all day in traffic jams or something."

The rain died off and there were patches of fog on the slopes of the mountains—clouds, I guess, that might later float on out over the dry plains to the east of us. I was thinking about rain when Walsh held up and I almost gouged a chunk out of my already scraped cheek on the tip of his rod.

"Ssssh! Look!"

Walsh pointed below us. The river here was running close to the trail, just down a steep slope from us, coming out of a riffle and dropping into a curving deep hole. There was a sandbar by the head of the pool, running along the far bank, even with my puffy eyes I could see it in the clear water, and then just below us the water was deep and gray-green and there was an uprooted tree and a logjam.

"Look!"

I followed Walsh's arm and looked into the river and my heart stopped. There was a long pause and then it went thud, and started again, racing. Right below us an immense brown trout swam up from the depths.

"That's the biggest fish I've ever seen in this river," Walsh said quietly.

"It's the biggest trout I've ever seen," I said. "It's as big as a salmon."

Really, it was. Even from our distance I thought I could make out the black spots on its back. It was a huge fish.

"Damn," Walsh said.

The brown cruised up out of the deep water, up into the shallows by the sandbar at the head of the pool—we could see it better there, silhouetted against the bright background. It was easily as big as any of the silver salmon I had caught on my Alaska trip. But it seemed nervous in the shallows, aware that we were watching, perhaps, and it turned and quickly disappeared into the deep water near the uprooted tree.

"Damn," Walsh said again.

I could feel my heart thumping in my chest. I noticed Cassie huddled up against me.

"Did you see it, hon?"

"Uh-huh."

I think she sounded impressed.

"Man, I'd love to catch a fish like that," Walsh said.

"Anybody would," I said thickly.

Walsh looked at me. I knew what he was thinking. He wanted that big brown—he wanted it right then. There would still be a couple or three hours of daylight left after he dropped me off with Patsy, plenty of time to come back and go for the big fish, but he wanted it right now. The fish was there, moving around. It was active. The moment was slipping. I knew what he was thinking, of course, because I was thinking the same thing. The thing was, he was capable of trying for the trout and I wasn't. I was just barely ambulatory—my face hurt, my brain was joggled, I was dizzy, I was bleeding, my casting hand was swollen. I was a mess, and Walsh was ready to go right then.

"Let's take a break," I said. "I need to sit down."

I grabbed hold of a tree branch and lowered myself to the damp ground. I was breathing heavily through my mouth—still trying not to pant. I really did need to take a break.

Walsh looked down at me. "I guess I'll have a try at that big one while you rest," he said. "Just a few casts."

I shrugged. "Sure."

"You tell me when you're ready to go, okay?"

Walsh hesitated. I got the impression that he was maybe a little uncomfortable leaving me to go fishing.

I said, "Okay."

"I'll just be a few minutes," Walsh said, and then he disappeared into the brush, heading upstream.

"Look out," I called after him. "Those rocks are slippery."

I didn't hear if he replied.

I moved a little, trying to make myself comfortable, and I looked down at the river, into the deep pool. Little pale mayflies were coming off the riffle above, drifting into the pool, and fish were rising there—and a couple of the fish seemed to be decent-sized. But I didn't think the big brown would be eating mayflies too often at this stage of her life—she was too big. She'd be eating the fish that were eating mayflies.

Cassie moved over close to me and I put my arm around her. I asked, "Where do you think the big one'll be?"

She shrugged. "I don't know."

"Probably under that big log pile," I said. "Hiding out, right?"

Walsh appeared below us then, wading out onto the sand bar. He tucked his rod under his arm and messed with his leader, tying on a new fly. After a minute or so he dropped the fly into the water and stripped some line from his reel. He looked like he was going to fish from where he stood, and I was surprised; it seemed that he could get a better float if he moved downstream a bit, casting from back in the tall grass. Of course, I was looking at it from a different angle than Walsh. Maybe he saw something I didn't.

Walsh looked behind him to see if there were any trees to hang up on, then made a roll-cast pickup and a couple of false casts, and dropped his fly against the bank below where Cassie and I were sitting.

"He's fishing a dry fly," I said.

"We were, before," Cassie said.

"Yeah," I said. "But I don't know, though. I think I'd run a big streamer down by those logs or something." I reached around Cassie and unzipped a pocket on my vest and pulled out a box of big deer-hair flies. "Or maybe one of these." I pulled out a cigar-shaped fly called a Bomber, designed for Atlantic salmon. I'd never fished for Atlantics, but I'd used Bombers in Texas for bass, and the ones I used were tied with heavy monofilament loops around the hook so that they wouldn't snag on logs.

Cassie took the fly and looked it over. Frowned. She said, "It's pretty big."

"It's a big fish," I said. "Let me see your rod."

She handed it to me and I snipped off the little Comparadun she'd been fishing and tied on the Bomber. I had to take my sunglasses off to see the leader, and when I did Cassie made a face and looked away.

"Hey!" she said.

I tightened the clinch knot—difficult with my jammed finger but not impossible—and looked up. Cassie was pointing at Walsh. He had a fish on—a pretty good one, too, it looked, though it wasn't the big one. After a few moments he netted it and held it up in our direction.

"It's a brown!" Walsh yelled. "Sixteen or eighteen inches!"

"Nice fish," I said to Cassie.

She nodded.

Walsh bent over and unhooked the fish and released it. He messed with his fly a bit and moved downstream, casting again, building up a solid rhythm. He was obviously an experienced fisherman but I still thought he was fishing too far from the log jam and the deep water.

I handed Cassie her rod. "Okay," I said. "When it's your turn I want you to cross the river up there at the sand bar and then go on down through that meadow and come up through the tall grass, to where you're right across from here. Okay?"

"We should probably just go," Cassie said.

"Huh-uh," I said. "I want to see if you can catch that big one. I bet you have a better chance of getting it than Walsh does."

I pointed out where Cassie should go again, and made her follow my arm where I pointed. Across the river and down, then back through the tall grass. I told her to keep low—to stay on her knees. Wait a few minutes for things to settle down. Then cast the Bomber as close to the log jam as she could, letting the current take it, let it drag and wake, try to annoy the big brown into coming up and smashing it. Cassie didn't seem too enthusiastic but she nodded at everything I said. I started getting excited—I really thought she had a chance.

Below us Walsh caught another brown, another nice fish for this little river but not as big as the other one. He released the fish, then stood up and waved at us, and disappeared upriver.

"You ready?" I asked Cassie.

"I think we should just go," Cassie said. She looked tired, and pale, and cold. She said, "Mom'll be waiting for us."

"Aw, c'mon," I said. I really wanted her to try for the big brown. It didn't seem like too much to ask. "Do this for me, all right?"

Cassie pursed her lips and stared straight ahead. Half-pouting. Walsh came up the trail grinning.

"That first one was a nice fish," Walsh said. He sat down next to me, heavily, and caught his breath.

"Yeah, I saw it," I said.

"You ready to take off?"

I shook my head. "Cassie wants a try at the big one."

"Huh!" Walsh laughed, a deep chesty cough. "What's she gonna do, drop a grenade down there or something?"

Cassie glared over at Walsh. She said, "I know how to fish." The sh on fish sounded almost like a hiss. I could tell she was pissed at Walsh. I put my hand on her shoulder and she shrugged it off. Maybe she was pissed at me, too.

Walsh looked suddenly sheepish. "Well, hey, give it a try. If your old man don't care."

I patted her on the knee. "Just do what I told you, hon, okay? We'll head back in a little bit."

Cassie stood up and hooked the Bomber into the hook-keeper on her rod and headed down toward the river. When her back was turned Walsh grinned at her and snorted, shaking his head. A light rain began falling again, and I pulled my jacket close around me and huddled back against the tree. I was wet and miserable and my face hurt. I wanted to go somewhere dry and warm where someone would take care of me—but even more, I wanted to wipe that grin off Walsh's face. I wanted to wipe it away even if I had to use my own daughter to do it.

"I didn't mean to piss her off, man," Walsh said, "but there's no way she's gonna catch that fish."

"She has a chance."

I spotted Cassie then, crossing the river at the shallow riffle. She went on up the bank and into the meadow, well back from the river, through the tall yellow grass. Then she turned and headed back our way, dropping to her hands and knees about halfway across, crawling the rest of the way to the river. She came out on the bank across from the log jam and looked up at us. The rain died off. So far she'd done everything just right.

Walsh snorted. "She gonna fish or what?"

"She has to rest the pool."

Walsh looked at me with that grin again. "What, you got that out of a book or something?"

Cassie was looking up at me from across the river. Finally I waved and nodded—and that hurt my head—and Cassie unhooked her Bomber and stripped some line from her reel. She fumbled with her equipment for a bit and then made a terrible sloppy cast and dropped the Bomber far short of the log jam. Walsh shook his head and I was embarrassed for her. Well, for me. But Cassie picked the fly up, made two false casts, and then dropped it where it was supposed to go, right next to the logs, over the undercut bank, over the deep green water. The river took the fly line and pulled the fly quickly along the front of the logs and out into the middle of the pool and on down.

"Too much drag," Walsh said.

"It's a waking fly," I said. "It's supposed to do that."

"These aren't bass," Walsh said.

Cassie made four more casts, all more or less on target. I was about ready to tell her to head on back when my heart stopped for the second time that day. I did not see the strike— I saw only a splash of water heading up and away from the logs, toward Cassie. But I knew what it was—the big brown—and my heart stopped. Cassie fell backwards, holding her rod high, her mouth open in surprise, and I pulled myself to my feet, and then— thump—my heart started beating again, and Cassie's rod was bowed over and she was on her feet and there was a tremendous splash in the river as the fish rolled and then Cassie was stupidly yanking on the slack line, trying hold on to the fish.

"Get it on the reel!" I yelled.

"She has to get it away from those logs," Walsh said.

I was already stumbling down the steep bank to the log jam. I slipped and fell—on my butt this time—and slid most of the way on the pine needles. Walsh was right behind me. Cassie's eyes were bugging out and her mouth was open in an O and her rod was surging and pulsing and the big brown was trying to get away—and then the rod went straight and the line fell back to her, all slack. The fish was gone.

"Goddamn it, Cassie," I yelled. "I told you to get that fish on the reel! What the hell were you trying to do?"

Cassie stood there staring at her slack line, amazed.

"Just what the hell were you trying to do?" I yelled again from across the river. My face was aching and my nose was bleeding again but I didn't care. "You could've caught that damn fish if you'd been paying attention!"

Cassie blinked and looked from the rod tip to me, and then at the water, trying to figure out what had happened. It was so quick. She stared at the log jam, at the river, lips pursed, breathing heavily, wet hair plastered to her forehead. After a moment she looked at me again, stony-eyed and panting, and then she reeled in her line, all of it, and ducked back into the grass.

"You can't go around doing that kind of shit," I yelled. I don't know if she heard me or not.

"There's no way she could've kept that big one out of the logs," Walsh said.

"Goddamn it," I said. I fell back against the soft bank, bleeding again from my forehead and my nose. I was out of breath and my heart was pounding.

I couldn't get over that fish. She should have had it.

A few minutes later Cassie came making her way through the brush. Her face was wet, though I think from the rain, and not from tears. She looked angry. But I was mad, too.

"Let's go," Cassie said.

"Let me see your rod," Walsh said.

She handed it to him wordlessly and he pulled the leader and some line off the reel and looked at it and shook his head.

"Hey, man," Walsh said to me. "There's no way she

could have caught that fish—you didn't bother to change the leader when you tied that big fly on. She was still using that little dry fly tippet. I'm surprised she could even cast that thing."

He reeled the line back in and handed the rod to Cassie. I looked at the rod in her hand.

Walsh said to me, "Man, you fucked that up."

Yeah, the tippet was too light.

I guess that was my fault.

But still.

"C'mon," Cassie said. "Let's go."

"Lighten up," I said. "My face hurts."

We were silent the rest of the way back to Walsh's truck. Walsh turned and looked at me occasionally—I couldn't read his glance—and when I turned to check on Cassie I saw that she was lagging behind. I forced a stop a couple of times to wait for her, and when she caught up she wouldn't say anything. Pouting. A child, still.

We found Walsh's truck and drove over the little pass and back to the campground—just about seven miles, like Cassie had said. Patsy was sitting at the table under the awning tinkering with her cameras when we got there, and she was shocked at my face, and more afraid of the blood than Cassie had been. We were able to calm her down, though—obviously I wasn't in any immediate danger of dying, not just now—and she grabbed her bag and our insurance information, and a change of clothes for us, and we piled back into Walsh's truck—Walsh and Patsy and myself jammed into the front, Cassie bouncing around with Walsh's empty beer cans in the back—for the ride back up to the river.

"He took one hell of a spill," Walsh told Patsy. "It was the damnedest thing I ever saw."

"He looks terrible," Patsy said. From the sound of her voice, she was scared. She didn't want to look at me but Walsh did, glancing over with both hands on the wheel, that damn grin on his face.

"Yeah!" Walsh said happily. "He looks like somebody just kicked his ass!"

I resisted the temptation to look at myself in the rearview mirror and just kept looking out the window, watching the damp, gray afternoon slide into evening. Everything reminded me of failure. Yeah, the leader was on me. But the fish was on Cassie. She could have caught it if she'd been paying attention.

Walsh came around a bend and there was my truck ahead of us. He pulled up behind it and cut the engine and I got out and stood there while he helped Cassie out of the back.

"You're a damn good little fisherman," Walsh said to her.

"Angler," Cassie said.

"Okay, whatever," Walsh said. "Still, I bet you'll go back and get that big brown, huh?"

Cassie shook her head, looking Walsh in the eye. "I don't want it," she said. "You can have it."

"Nah, it's yours. Go back and get it tomorrow." He clapped her on the shoulder. "Just don't pay attention to what your old man says and you'll do fine."

Patsy unlocked our truck and opened the door and Cassie darted around me and hopped up in the front seat.

I faced Walsh. "Hey, thanks for helping, you—"

Walsh waved me off, grinning. "Just get to a doctor, man. You look like shit." He backed away, still grinning at me—like I was a greenhorn, like I was stupid. A tourist.

Maybe I was stupid.

Patsy put our gear in the truck and started it, and I got in, sitting next to Cassie. Walsh pulled around us, tooting his horn, disappearing around a bend in the road.

"You're lucky he was there," Patsy said. "You're very lucky."

I didn't answer. Yeah, I was lucky. I guess maybe I was lucky. Patsy carefully turned the truck around and we headed back the way we came, past the campground and across a bridge—I looked down at the river and thought of the big trout just upstream from us, thought of that cold water I'd been in. I leaned against the door, drained.

"Dad took my shirt," Cassie said suddenly.

Patsy glanced over at me. My headband, Cassie's shirt, was caked with blood and dirt.

"We'll get you a new shirt," Patsy said. "I think I got you clean clothes for tonight."

We turned onto the highway and headed east. Patsy pointed at a moose standing in a beaver pond but I wasn't interested. We were going down out of the mountains. I was getting drowsy but every time I nodded off my head bumped against the window and my face hurt.

"I don't ever want to go fishing again," Cassie said.

"No, that's okay," I said. "I don't think you should."

The Point

The car rolled to a stop on the packed snow in front of my mother's house and I sat there for a moment, looking out the windshield. The night was clear and cold, and there were little halos around porch lights on houses up and down the street.

"You want to wait here or come in?" I asked. "I'll just be a minute."

"Too cold," Corrine said. She was unbuckling her seat belt. "Anyway, I want to meet your mom."

We got out of the car and when the car doors shut they sounded very loud. It was a quiet night. Most of the houses along the street had some sort of lights strung up outside, and they were all quietly pulsing green or red or blue, and almost every house had the curtains on the front windows open, and you could look in and see their Christmas trees, all lit up and sparkly.

"What a pretty night," Corrine said. She kicked at the snow.

The sidewalk in front of the house was barely shoveled. We went up the driveway and I bent over and tried the garage door. It was locked, and I had lost my key.

"Well," I said. "So much for sneaking in."

We went around the front of the house, passing in front of the big picture window. The Christmas tree blocked most of it, but I could see my mom in there, sitting back in her recliner and watching TV. There was a big green bottle of gin on the table beside her. I could just barely hear the sound of the TV through the walls of the house.

I rang the bell and banged hard on the door two or three times. The sound of the TV disappeared and I could see a shadow moving in the living room—my mother getting out of the recliner and coming to the door. The porch light came on.

I looked back at Corrine. There wasn't anything to say.

There was some fumbling at the lock and then the door opened. My mother looked at me for a moment.

"Oh," she said, surprised for a second. "Well, hi there!"

"Hi," I said. I stepped past her into the house. It was very warm inside and everything smelled heavily of pine—it smelled like Christmas, I guess. I turned around. "Uh, Mom, this is Corrine. Corrine—my mom."

"Hi," Corrine said. "I've been wanting to meet you for a long time."

"Well, aren't you a beauty!" My mother looked Corrine over, smiling, and then hugged her. Corrine looked over my mom's shoulder and arched her eyebrows at me, smiling. She thought this was funny. My mom said, "Come on in and sit down. I was just watching the news."

Corrine broke away from my mother, unzipping her coat. She looked around the room.

"What a pretty tree," Corrine said.

My mom waved her hand. "I just threw on a bunch of stuff we had when the kids were little. Anyway, it's kind of lopsided, don't you think?" She reached over and straightened the tree maybe a little.

"Looks fine to me."

Mom settled back into her recliner. "Would you like a drink?" she asked Corrine. "I was having a drink while I was watching the news."

"We just stopped in for a second," I said. "I just need to—"

"Sure," Corrine said. She took off her coat and muffler and sat in the big gray chair facing the TV.

Mom got back up and went into the kitchen. I looked at Corrine. She smiled at me.

"Your mom's nice."

I said, "Yeah?"

Mom quickly came out with a glass and some ice.

"I was having a drink while I was watching the news," she said again. She squinted at me—her eyes were very bright—like I wasn't even there, really.

"Uh, I just need to get something out of my bedroom," I said. I took a step toward the stairs.

"Doug," Mom said, and I stopped. She slopped some gin—a lot of gin, really a lot—into the glass and handed it to Corrine. Then she looked up at me. "I just realized your father was an alcoholic. I just realized that tonight. The news had a special report on the cost of alcoholism and I realized that your dad was one."

"Oh," I said. I looked back at her and shrugged big. I couldn't think of anything else to say.

"It's true," Mom said. "He was. He was just like those drunk people on TV."

"Well," I said, and stopped. I looked over at Corrine: she was gazing into her glass of gin. I said, "I guess it's too late to do anything about it, now."

"I just thought you should know," Mom said.

"Thanks," I said. "I need to get something out of my room. I turned and headed up the stairs.

"Doug's father was such a wonderful man, in so many ways," I could hear mom say to Corrine. "But he did like to go to Happy Hour...."

I went down the hall to my old bedroom. Just as I

opened the door, I noticed a light coming from beneath the door of my sister's room. I stepped over and knocked on her door.

I heard someone say, "Fuck."

Then my sister said, "Who is it?"

"It's me, damn it." I banged on the door again. Kait had quit school and moved back home a week or so earlier, and I hadn't seen her in a while.

"Wait a sec." I could hear her moving around, and then the door opened. Kait was looking a tad blurred. "When'd you get here?"

I stepped past her into the room. It was thick with marijuana smoke. I looked at her and laughed. "Holy shit!"

"You want some?" Kait's friend Monica offered me a joint.

"Nah, not right now." I looked at Kait. "So what's up?"

"Just sitting around."

"I guess," I said. "I just stopped in for a minute to get something. I left Corrine downstairs with mom."

"You brought Corrine here? I want to see what she looks like."

"She just looks like—Corrine." I shrugged and looked around.

"I want to see her." Kait was grinning at me. She picked up a dirty glass. "I think I'll go downstairs and get some pop."

"Oh, c'mon. Poor Corrine's gonna think she's in a zoo."

"She is," Kait said. She left the room.

Monica was staring hard at me. High. She said, "Your ma's pretty loaded tonight."

"Yeah, no kidding."

I left Kait's room and went next door to my old room. It wasn't really used for anything now—my mother was using it to store things, junk mostly—but I still had a lot of stuff in it. I turned the light on and opened the closet and pulled out a few boxes and spread them across my mother's sewing table. The second box I opened had my Indian stuff in it, a wooden cigar box of arrowheads and broken flint tools, and one spear point, a nice one, about the size of the palm of my hand, made of dark flint, richly fluted. I had found it sticking out of a dirt clod in the middle of a cut down cornfield one day when I was pheasant hunting with my dad. I don't remember how old I was then—eleven or twelve, maybe, just big enough to carry a .410 and keep up with the men. I fell to my knees and tugged it out of the soil and held it up, yelling for my father to come see. He hurried over and was happy for me, and Stewart, the pointer, stuck his nose next to my face, and the sky was high and clear and blue like it is sometimes in the fall. My father wondered about the man who had made the point, and how it had come to be where it was. He told me I was very, very lucky. I always remembered his face that day, and the sky, and the metallic sheen of the pheasant's covert feathers, and the hard sharpness of the flint in my hand.

Now the point was cold and heavy in my hand. I squeezed it tight and felt the still-sharp edges dig at my soft palm. It was really a very beautiful thing.

After a moment I looked around in the closet some more and found a hard plastic box that a wristwatch had once come in, and then I put everything else back into the closet. I placed the point in the box and went back into Kait's room.

"That was quick," Monica said.

"I knew what I was looking for," I said. Kait had a pile of People magazines that went back years—decades, at least. She collected them at flea markets and used them for collages and miscellaneous room-clutter. I dug around in one of the stacks and pulled a copy out from near the bottom. Just right. The long-dead Princess of Wales was on the cover. I tore the front cover off the magazine and took some tape from Deb's desk and began wrapping the box.

Kait came back into the room carrying a can of Diet

Coke. She asked, "What're you doing?"

"He's tearing up your magazines," Monica said.

Kait looked over my shoulder at the dead Princess's face. She said, "Bitch."

"What's his girlfriend like?" Monica asked.

"She's a babe," Kait said. "I'd even go for her."

"I'm glad you approve," I said. I folded the last end of the wrapping paper and tore off a bit of tape.

"She's got real sharp, bright eyes," Kait said to Monica. "Long dark hair. Nice smile. She's hot."

"Excellent," Monica said.

I didn't say anything. Kait looked at me.

"So, what's in the box?" she asked. "You giving her a present?"

"Yep."

"What is it, a watch?"

"Nope."

"It's a ring," Monica said.

Kait looked at her. "Could be. Dad gave Doug the wedding rings when him and mom got divorced. He stashed them away somewhere."

"It's not a ring," I said. "Jesus."

"It's more like a pendant thing or something," Monica said. "Like a planet she can wear around her neck—you know, like a Saturn or something."

"What?" I looked at her like she was crazy. She was just high, though.

Kait said, "Or a comet!"

"Yeah," Monica said. "Or a comet or something to wear around her neck. Man, I'd like one of those, you know?"

I left them smoking more dope and went back down the stairs. The living room was empty, and the TV was on with the sound turned off. The bottle of gin was almost empty. I heard some voices and went down the hall to the kitchen. Corrine and my mother were there, drinks in hand, laughing about something.

My mom looked up and saw me. "Oh, there you are," she said. "We've been talking about your father. I was just showing Corrine where he threw me through the wall."

I frowned. That was a lie, probably. At least, it was something I'd never heard of before, and I'd actually lived with them for 15 goddamn years. And how do you throw somebody through a wall? Wouldn't you hit a 2x4 or something?

I asked, "So when was this supposed to happen?"

Corrine looked at me and shook her head, No. Do not.

"And then I had to tell her about the time your father was drunk and emptied a bottle of barbecue sauce over your head when you were—what?—nine or ten."

"It wasn't barbecue sauce," I said. I was pretty sure he wasn't drunk, either, but I didn't say anything. Even in memory, his sobriety had made that dark anger all the more frightening. "It was Worcestershire sauce."

For some reason Corrine thought that was funny.

I didn't say anything. I was suddenly pissed—my mother could never, ever, tell a straight story. Everything she said came out twisted and distorted to serve herself, the poor damn victim. Everything was a lie.

"But the thing is, Doug," my mom said. "This little girl doesn't know anything about our family. What have you been telling her?"

I paused. I could feel myself getting red in the face. I took a breath. I finally said, "Nothing."

"Well, obviously."

Corrine laughed again. She put her hand over her mouth and glanced at me, then looked back at the floor. What the fuck was her problem all of a sudden?

"We probably ought to go," I said to her. "We'll be late for the movie."

"Doug likes to think that he's punctual," Mom said.

"Yeah," I said. "That's true. I don't like to be late."

"Little Doug was always rushing us around," Mom said. "He'd go, 'Take me to Cub Scouts,' 'take me swimming.'

He was always whining about being on time, like we lived in a damn train station or something, or an airport."

Mom tossed back the last of her drink. She looked around, a little befuddled, and then reached over and placed the glass in the sink.

"Okay," Corrine said. "Let's go."

"Stick around," Mom said. She opened a cabinet and brought out another big green bottle of gin.

"No, we have to go," I said. I made a face at Corrine and turned and started back down the hall. I heard her following along behind me.

"Stick around," my mom called again.

I stopped in front of the Christmas tree to watch Corrine put on her coat.

I said, "This is what it is."

Corrine looked at me, her chin down as she zipped up. "It's okay."

"No," I said. "Really, I'm sorry."

I didn't know what to do. I was stuck. I looked around the room—silent TV, the chair, the empty green bottle, the tree. Pictures on the wall—me, Kait. Corrine stood tugging at her jacket zipper and I stood there looking around. This is what it was. I stood there and watched my mother come down the hall carrying the gin bottle. She plopped back in her chair and refilled her glass.

"I hate to see you kids just leave," she said. "I just hate spending these nights alone."

"Kait and Monica are upstairs," I said.

"Yeah, well." She rolled her eyes. "Those girls."

"We don't want to be late for the movie," Corrine said.

"Well, I suppose."

I pulled the car keys out of my pocket. "Okay, then. We'll catch you later."

"Good-bye," Corrine said.

My mother suddenly saw the box in my hand. "What's that? A present?"

I held the door open and Corrine was going through it.

"Yeah, it's a present."

"It was nice meeting you!" Corrine called past me. She was out on the steps and I could feel the nice cool air rush past her into the house.

Mom got out of her chair and came over to the door. "Tell me what it is." She reached out to take the box from me.

"It's none of your goddamn business what it is," I said flatly.

"Come on, you can tell me."

"Oh, go to hell." I shut the door in her face. I looked at Corrine, who was standing below me on the steps. "Well, that's over."

She didn't say anything. My mother appeared in the picture window, next to the tree. She had her hand on the glass and was peering out at us. Corrine waved.

I said, "Let's get the fuck out of here."

We walked down the driveway and back to my car. It was very quiet out and the snow under our feet squeaked and crunched.

Corrine said, "You shouldn't talk to your mother that way."

There was a streetlight behind her and when she exhaled her breath came out in a big, glowing cloud.

I looked past her back into the darkness and didn't say anything. She didn't know what she was talking about. I hit the button to unlock the car for her and then opened the driver's side door.

Corrine said, "It's not very nice."

I got in the car. Corrine was buckling her seatbelt and didn't look at me. I tossed the box onto her lap.

I said, "Merry Christmas."

Multiflora Rose

One afternoon I was sitting at the Derrick Lounge with my back to the door, watching Sportscenter on the barroom TV, drinking the afternoon away, when someone covered my eyes from behind and kissed me, wet and warm, on the neck. I was startled — this wasn't the kind of greeting I expected at the Derrick. Or anywhere. I lurched forward, trying to tear free from the hands over my eyes, dropping my newspaper, knocking over my beer, half falling off my stool. I finally wrenched around and stood up, and there was Faye Reed, smiling at me.

"You're awful jumpy," Faye said. "What're you so afraid of?"

"Nothing," I said. I looked around the bar. Carey the barmaid had been playing one of the poker machines, and there were two old guys sitting down at the far end of the bar, sipping redeyes. All three were turned around watching me with some sort of slippery befuddled amusement. I looked back at Faye.

"When'd you get back?" I asked.

"Just now," she said. "I stopped by your place and you weren't home but your truck was there, so I figured you'd be someplace close."

"Came down for lunch," I said.

Faye said, "You're just getting to be an old drunk."

I shrugged. "Not much else to do around here."

She walked around me—erect, tightly muscled, lithe—and sat on a stool with her back to everyone else.

I asked, "Been to see Craig yet?"

"No." Faye shook her head and looked above the bar at the TV. I followed her gaze. A couple of guys arguing about quarterbacks. Football season hadn't even started yet. Faye said, "I suppose I'll have to—I'm going to be here for the whole weekend. Makes me sad."

I bent over and picked up my newspaper. I saw a dime on the floor and picked it up, too. I slid it across the bar to Faye.

"Welcome home," I said. "You might need this."

Faye pushed the coin back and forth on the bar with her fingertips. "You want to go with me to see him?" she asked. "You can talk to Daddy—he always did like you."

Before I could say anything Carey finished her poker game and came around the bar, picking up a wet bar rag on the way.

"Bill, Bill, you make such a mess," she said, wiping at my spilled beer. She looked at Faye, trying to place her. "Hey."

Faye smiled. "Can you get him another beer, please? And one for me, too?"

"Sure." Carey went up the bar. She pulled out two bottles of Budweiser and rang them up, watching Faye the whole time. When she brought the beers over, she said, "Didn't you marry Kenny Hyre?"

Faye looked at me and made a face.

"You can't every live anything down," I said. "Everybody remembers everything."

"I guess so," Faye said. She pulled some money from her pocket and paid for the beers. She said to Carey, "Yeah. That didn't work out, though."

"Oh—I'm sorry to hear that."

"Oh, don't be!"

Carey shrugged and moved off to the cash register. I shrugged, too. No reason for anybody to be sorry about that breakup. Kenny was a mess..

*

We left the bar and crossed Main Street. It was a slow August afternoon, and there were few people moving about. Downtown had been falling apart since they expanded the strip mall out on Highway 5, and the grocery store had closed, and the pharmacy, and the dress shop, and the feed store. Even the time and temperature sign on the bank was broke.

"I like living in Columbus," Faye said. "It's big. There's all these people around, and you hardly ever see anybody you know."

"You probably wouldn't know that many people around here anymore, either," I said.

A pickup truck passed us, going up the hill to the courthouse. The sun was on the back of our heads and was hot, and cicadas were buzzing in the trees Faye walked along with her face tilted back, her eyes half-closed, and I couldn't tell if she noticed the cicadas, or me, or the pickup truck.

"So you're still teaching, right?" She opened her eyes and glanced at me. "Adjuncting."

"They got me teaching a section of economics this second summer session," I said. "In the fall they've got me down for three sections of Intro to Accounting."

"I'm surprised you stayed here this long." Faye looked away, up the hill toward the college.

"Shoot—you're surprised." I really needed to finish my dissertation. I really needed to go somewhere and find a real job, full-time with benefits.

"You're never going to leave here," Faye said.

We turned the corner and headed down Howard Street to my little house. The county courthouse and the jail were at the top of a steep grassy slope just above my place, and in the evenings the lone guard at the jail would sit out on the cool grass and clean his pistol.

"And you're living in town, now," Faye said. "I heard you got the farm rented out."

"Yeah," I said, "I've got the place up for sale, too, but nobody's even come by to look at it."

"That's such a shame. Your family was there all those years."

"They're all gone now," I said. "Even the apple trees died."

Faye's big black Trans Am was parked next to my truck. A note was fluttering on my door. BILL, it said, WHERE ARE YOU? FAYE, with a little heart drawn around the Faye.

"I left that for you," she said.

"No kidding?" I unlocked the door and we went inside.

Faye looked around my living room. She said, "Well, at least you're still a pig."

I shrugged and went on into the kitchen to get beers. When I came back Faye was standing in front of my computer, trailing her left forefinger along the keyboard. She was looking at the wall above the machine, at a photo: Faye and myself, my sister and her boyfriend, all of us drunk and cheerful at Blackwater Falls.

"I can't believe how young I was then."

"You're not old, now."

Faye quickly turned and hugged me, and I had to lean kind of sideways to place the beers on the desk before I was able to put my arms around her.

"You're sweet," she said. Then, after a moment, "I'm glad you're here, to talk to Daddy. I never know what to say to him alone."

I looked away and frowned. The last time I'd seen Faye's father was over at the little general store in Burnt

House. I was standing behind him, and he didn't know I was there, and he was telling the other men how his daughter would turn up her ass for any man with drugs. Someone signaled him and he turned and greeted me like he'd said nothing shameful, nothing. No sign of embarrassment.

"Your dad's not real easy to talk to," I said.

"He's an asshole," Faye said.

"That, too."

Faye pulled away from me then and took one of the beers and sat down on the couch, looking at me brightly.

"Well," she said. "Here we are."

I sat down next to her on the couch. She put her head on my shoulder and I moved and put my arm around her.

Faye sighed. "God, everything's been so weird."

She looked up at me and I kissed her. When we broke apart she looked at me. Her eyes were very light and shiny—teary, just about crying.

"I've missed you, Bill," she said.

"Well, I've missed you, too," I said.

We kissed again and I fell backward on the couch and pulled her atop me. Her pale brown hair was down over my face and she was smiling, kissing me on the neck and cheek, and I pulled her t-shirt up and over her head, her hair popping through at the last instant, Faye laughing, and then unhooking her bra, holding her close, soft and warm. I kissed the freckles on her shoulders.

"No," Faye said after a minute.

"No?"

"No," she said, "really, I don't want to. Just hold me for a little bit."

Faye put her head on my chest, her hair splaying out over me. I moved my head a little so the hair wouldn't tickle my nose.

"I know what you think about me," she said.

I said, "I think pretty good things about you."

"Sure you do." I could hear her breathing, could feel

her breath on my chest. "I know what men think."

After a while she looked up, shaking the hair from her face, and kissed me on the lips.

"We should probably go see Craig," she said. Her breath was sweet and heavy. I shut my eyes and didn't say anything.

Faye slid off me and sat up and looked around for her clothes. I opened my eyes and watched her get dressed, and she looked at me as she bent over, struggling into her bra.

"Are you okay?" she asked.

I shrugged. "I guess so."

Faye smiled thinly. "I know what you're thinking." She squeezed my thigh and got up and walked across the room.

✳

"You better drive," Faye said. "I'm tired."

Faye handed me the keys to her car and patted me on the shoulder, and I walked around to the driver's side and got in. Faye got in the other side and rolled down her window.

"It's so weird being back here," she said. "It's like nothing ever changes."

"Oh, things change here," I said. I started the car. "Things just change slower, is all."

"That's the same as no change, silly."

I thought about that. "Well, change is bad, anyway."

"Now you sound like Daddy."

Well. There was no good answer to that. I backed the car around and drove down Howard Street and turned up Court, heading up and over the hill, through the college campus. Some boys were in front of the dorm throwing a football around.

"I thought about taking some classes at CCSC," Faye said. "But I figured it'd be too much trouble. Then I got that job at the bank, and that takes all my time." She looked over at me. "When're you going to finish your dissertation?"

There was no answer to that, either. I shrugged. I said, "Someday, I guess."

I drove north out of town, up Grass Run and over the hill. The hills were dark and green and the air was moist. Here and there through the trees you could see nice, clean pastures and cattle, but many farms were abandoned— people living in the houses, perhaps, but the fields were all grown up thick with brush, and on many places timber was taking over and squeezing out the brush.

"Everything's so green," Faye said.

"You come by our old place on the way in?" I asked.

She shook her head. "I came in on Route Five. Forty-seven's too rough anymore."

"It's all grown up," I said. I glanced at her and back at the road. "We've got trees growing out of the pasture. There'll be squirrel hunting there in a few years."

"It's pretty," she said. "All the trees."

We followed Leading Creek for a while, then turned and followed Cove Creek, heading upstream. Cicadas were buzzing in the big sycamores along the road, and briars and vines were hanging down from the trees, crossing the road in some places like leafy curtains. Cool air blew in through the windows and whipped Faye's hair. She leaned her head out the window and shut her eyes and smiled as the wind hit her face. After a while she reached out and tried to grab hold of a vine hanging from a sugar tree.

"Ouch!" Faye said. "Damn."

I looked over and she was holding her hand and forearm. There were long scratches on her palm, and blood. Most of the pretty green vines were thorny greenbrier or multiflora rose.

I said, "That was kind of stupid."

"No kidding." She turned and rooted around in the back seat and found a rag of some sort and wrapped it around her hand. She didn't say anything for a while, and just sat looking out the window at the hillsides.

"You okay?" I finally asked.

"Stings a little," she said.

✻

We crossed the low-water bridge and went on up a hill to the Reed place. I could see Faye's father, Buddy, working on the side of a hill with a scythe, mowing a path through the brush. He stopped working when he saw the car, and stood wiping the sweat from his face. Faye leaned out the window and waved.

I pulled up next to the barn. A fat beagle came out from around the house and barked at us a few times and then sat and scratched at her ear. The lawn was smooth and green and well-kept and there was plenty of shade from a huge weeping willow. A little boy came out on the porch and stood leaning shyly against the banister.

"Oh, gosh, there he is," Faye said. She put her hand on my arm and bit her lower lip.

"Well," I said.

Before his birth and for several months after it, I had the idea that Craig might be my son. But Faye had denied it long enough and angrily enough that I decided to take her word for it. Craig didn't look too much like a Ramsey, anyway, though he was a pretty little boy, with red hair and freckles. Faye never told me who the father was, and she left the boy behind with her parents when she married Kenny Hyer and moved to Ohio.

Faye took her hand off my arm and got out of the car and stood looking at her son. I got out, too, and saw Buddy coming off the hill with his scythe. Faye looked across the roof of the car at me.

She asked, "What do we do now?"

I said, "Hell, I don't know."

Buddy hung his scythe over the fence and came

through the gate and over to us. He wasn't wearing a shirt and his powerful shoulders were covered with curly gray hair. Broken bits of leaves and flowers dusted his chest.

"Hey, Bill," he said, slowly, nodding at me. "Fayette."

"Hi, Daddy," she said. "Where's Mom?"

"She went over to see Mrs. Pendergrast," Buddy said. "She's got lymphoma."

"Oh yeah?" I asked. "I saw in the paper where'd she's been in the hospital."

Buddy looked past me to the house. "Craig!" he yelled. "Come over here and talk to your mother."

The little boy stepped off the porch and slowly walked over to us. The fat beagle got up and trotted along after him.

"Your yard looks real nice," I said to Buddy. "Looks like you've been working hard."

"Goddamn multiflora rose," Buddy said. He walked back toward the fence and I followed him, hoping to give Faye a little more space when she talked to Craig. There was a khaki work shirt hanging from the gate and Buddy put it on but didn't button it, his big belly sticking out gray-haired and round and hard. He fished a crumpled package of cigarettes from the front pocket of the shirt and pointed up the hill with his chin. "Been trying to keep a right-of-way open up to my TV antenna. Damn multiflora rose keeps coming back."

"It's pretty thick most places anymore," I said. Just something to say. I was watching Faye and Craig, though. She had her hands on his thin shoulders and was holding him at arm's length, talking to him quietly. The beagle was jumping up, trying to pull the bloody rag off her arm. I had a sudden urge to gather Faye up, along with the boy—and the dog, too, for that matter—and take them all away, to wherever Faye wanted to go, back to Columbus if that's what she wanted, or to Akron or Cincinnati or even Cleveland, and I could finish my dissertation, find a teaching job somewhere, take care of everybody, just pack up and head out across the Ohio River and keep on going West until we found someplace new. Right? Run away.

Just that easy!

"Hell," Buddy said. I stopped and looked back at him. He lit a cigarette and sniffed. "I remember when they brought that multiflora rose into this country. Department of Agriculture brought it in, said it'd make a fine natural fence. Now it's run wild everywhere."

Buddy had been looking up the hill toward the tangle of deep green brush. Now he turned and looked at me, and then at his daughter and grandson.

Buddy said, "This country's been ruined."

A Real Emergency

One of my earliest alleged memories is from when we lived out in the country, my parents and me, it was before my little brother was born, and one time a neighbor brought over a couple of rabbits he'd shot. I was three years old at the time, or maybe four, and I went into serious hysterics at the sight of the dead, limp rabbits. I've been told that I was crying and screaming and carrying on until it was past my bedtime, and then I was having bad dreams, waking up and screaming again. I never forgot it.

Well—of course, one of the reasons I never forgot it was that my goddamn parents never let me forget it. As long as they lived, and they lived a long time, they teased me about the rabbits. "This is Todd," my Mom or Dad would say. "He's the one that's afraid of dead rabbits." And everyone—anyone they told—would laugh at me. It was something I thought I couldn't live down until after my parents were as dead as those rabbits. Of course, even after they died, it still bothered me. I never lived it down, and wouldn't. I was stuck with the dead rabbits—I'm stuck with them now.

You never live anything down.

But then one day my wife, Candy, texted me an hour or so before I got off work.

Theres an emergency--get home asap

Just that text.

There was an emergency—but she didn't say what kind of emergency. She just said to get on home as soon as I could.

She didn't say anything about dead animals.

I looked at the text, and I thought—well, I thought. I assumed that Christa, our daughter, was safe. Candy would have said if Christa had been hit by a car or kidnapped or was sick or something. So then I guessed that the emergency was something along the order of a leaky pipe or a clogged drain or a wasp in the kitchen—and, listen, Candy can get hysterical over shit like that—and so I took my time and went on to one more dull meeting with the branch analyst and the training coordinator, and then I checked my phone again—no more texts—and then I cleaned off my desk, and I drove on home.

No rush, right? It wasn't a real emergency.

I parked my car in the driveway and I got out, carrying my jacket and briefcase, and walked over to look at these pink and yellow roses I'd planted along the front of the house. They were dry. Everything needed watering.

"Todd!" Candy's voice was low but emphatic.

I looked up. Candy was standing in the doorway, her hair all stressed and mussed.

"Hey, hon," I said. "I came as quick as I could."

"You didn't come quick enough," Candy hissed. She looked over her shoulder and then came out onto the steps. "Christa's already home from school."

"Well, good."

"No, it's not good," Candy whispered. "Your fish died."

"What?" The fish died? Then I thought, Oh, the fish in the aquarium. But there was more than one fish. One was dead, though. Okay. It happened. I asked, "Which one?"

"That bass—the big one."

"Well, that's too bad," I said.

I tried to put my arm around Candy's shoulder and squeeze her, sort of a hug, but Candy pulled away.

"I wanted you to come and get rid of it before Christa got home," Candy said. "If she sees it she'll get upset."

"Well, yeah." I shrugged. I could see that, sort of. I've had those rabbits in my brain forever. Though I also thought it would kind of depend—I mean, it was a fish, not a cat. Not a rabbit. It wasn't even a fucking mammal. I said, "I guess."

Candy stood close to me and whispered, "Christa was very attached to that fish."

"Well," I said. "Okay. I'll see what I can do."

I went up the steps and into the house. And then I really thought—Hey, this is my chance to do it right. Not be like my mom and dad. Candy was already upset— mad, nervous, something—and Christa still didn't know what was going on. This was my chance to take care of everybody and not leave anybody feeling bad.

Christa was sitting in front of the television, eating chips and playing a video game. She was shooting at something.

"Hey, kid," I said.

"What?" Christa asked.

"Hey, kid," I said again. I tossed my briefcase on a chair and laid my jacket over the back of it. Candy came in and made a little gesture with her hand, pointing toward the back of the house. I nodded—but I wanted to say something to Christa. Just be friendly. A dad. I asked her, "You learn anything at school today?"

"What?" Christa asked. She was staring at the screen, shooting at—things. Zombies, maybe. Things. Then she said, "No."

"Well, maybe someday you will." I looked at the TV for a moment.

"What?" Christa asked.

"Todd," Candy said. She put her hand at the small of my back and pushed.

"Yeah, okay." I went down the hallway to Candy's office, which was also where we kept the aquariums. Candy's desk and computer—she was a freelance public relations consultant— took up half the room. The three aquariums were at the back of the room, along the wall, sharing shelf space with my fly tying equipment. Two of the aquariums had the usual guppies and swordtails, but the third held—had held—two largemouth bass, Annette and Tony. I'd caught them while fishing in the lake here in the middle of town, fingerlings, baby bass so small they were barely the size of the fly I was using. They were cute, and so I decided to keep them. I brought them home in an ice chest and put them in an aquarium, and for the next year or so I fed them on bugs from the yard, mealworms from the baitshop, and an occasional guppy or swordtail. I think at first I had the idea of studying their habits to become a better fisherman, but then I ended up just liking them because they were interesting. And then I sort of forgot about them, or got used to them. I fed them and that was about it.

"I haven't been able to get any work done all day," Candy said. "Just knowing that dead thing was in here with me."

I knew she was telling the truth. Candy was like that. She had things to do and probably hadn't been able to get anything done. That might be silly. I don't know. I guess I thought it probably was. I wasn't going to get freaked out over a dead fish.

From the other side of the room I could see that the dead fish was Annette. She was slightly longer than Tony, and bulkier. She was bobbing belly up in the tank, her pectoral fins breaking the water. Tony finned calmly in the bottom of the tank, holding next to a large rock. I felt sorry for him, all alone.

I said, "I wonder why she died."

"Who cares? It just died," Candy sat down in the chair in front of her desk and spun around to watch me. "I just want her—it—out of my office without Christa knowing about it, you know?"

"Yeah." I looked around. "Why don't you go get me a plastic bag or something?"

"What for?"

"I'll put the fish in it and throw it in the trash."

Candy lit a cigarette and shook her head, blowing smoke at me. "Huh-uh," she said. "The trash doesn't go out till Thursday. It'll start stinking before then."

"Well, then, I'll take it out back and bury it."

Candy shook her head again. "The cat will dig it up, or a dog will come along, or something."

I sat down in a chair and looked at Candy. She'd had all day to think up solutions to the dead fish problem. She'd passed through two or three stages over the course of the day, right: shock, then grossed-outedness, then solution. Candy was holding something back. She had an idea. I waited. She waited, too. We looked at each other.

Finally, I asked, "Well, what do you want me to do? Drive it out to the damn landfill and drop it off?"

Candy shrugged like she didn't care. She said, "I guess that would work."

"Come on," I said. "I'm not gonna drive thirty miles for a dead fish. Might as well flush it down the toilet."

I wanted to do everything right, but I didn't want to spend the rest of my day messing with a dead fish.

"Todd," Candy said. "You're going to do this for me. I don't care where you take it, but you're going to get that fish out of this house."

And she was serious. She meant it. And so I backed down, or pretended to.

"What the hell," I said.

I decided I'd flush it down the toilet. I've flushed grosser things than dead fish.

Candy asked, "But what do we do about Christa when you're carrying that thing to the car?"

"Oh, shit, I don't know," I said. "You want her out of the house? Go take her to the store or something. Go get a pizza or some chicken or something. Or fish."

"No fish," Candy said. She stood up and went out of the room. She called, "Hey, Chrissy!"

I sat there and watched the aquariums. Tony the surviving bass was holding next to his rock below the stream of bubbles from the aerator. Poor lonely fish. I wondered what I'd do if Candy suddenly died. Get her out of the house before she started to stink, I suppose. Don't let Christa know. But she'd have to know—

I heard a noise and turned around. Candy came in with a plastic bag, and I laughed.

"What's so funny?"

I took the bag from her and unfolded it. It was a 39 gallon lawn and leaf bag.

I said, "The fish is only about five inches long."

"Well, I don't know what you're going to do with it— maybe wrap it up or something." Candy folded her arms across her chest. "I don't really want to know, either. I'm going to tell Christa that it went to visit its Mother in the lake."

"I think a second grader can handle a dead fish," I said. But in a way, I wasn't so sure. There were those rabbits I cried about when I was a kid, right. But the problem there wasn't the dead rabbits, of course, it was my parents.

And I wasn't like them. I wasn't going to be like them.

And, anyway, Christa was older now than I was then. She saw dead things on TV all the time. She'd be okay.

Candy called from the front of the house, "We're going!"

"Okay!" I called back.

I draped the huge plastic bag over the back of a chair, and then I rolled up my shirt sleeve and opened the top of the aquarium. I reached in and after a moment—after an almost flinch—I stuck my hand in the tank and the water was cold, and she was cold and dead. It was a little gross. I lifted her from the water, holding her for a moment to let the water run off her tail back into the tank. Didn't want to make a mess. The surviving fish, Tony, drifted up from the bottom, thinking it might be feeding time— or, I thought, maybe he's saying goodbye. Looking at Tony bothered me somehow, and I quickly turned and carried Annette out of the room and across the hall into our bedroom, and into the bathroom that opened off the bedroom.

I lifted the toilet seat with my foot and held Annette over the bowl.

"You were a good fish," I said. "I named you after the most incompetent employee I ever had, and you served me better than she ever did." I thought for a minute. "I'm kind of sorry I brought you out of the lake. But here at least you didn't get eaten by your Mother."

Then I pushed the lever, and as the water swirled I dropped Annette tail-first into the toilet, and shut the lid.

Success. No tears shed—not by me, not by my kid.

I dozed off, stretched out on the bed in the darkened room, and woke up with a start when Candy and Christa came home. I heard them talking in the kitchen, and tried to go back to sleep, but it was no use, and I was awake with my eyes closed when Candy came into the room. She grabbed my left big toe and squeezed it.

"Hey," I said.

"Oh, you're awake."

"Sort of."

"We got pizzas," Candy said. "Go get something to eat."

"Later," I said. I rolled over and grabbed at Candy's arm and pulled her down onto the bed.

"No!" Candy said. She sat back up, brushing the hair

from her eyes. "I've got some work to catch up on. Go on out and talk to Christa or something."

"Later," I said. I pulled a pillow over my face.

Candy stood up. "Well, sleep, then."

"I'm sleeping," I said.

Candy stepped into the bathroom, and yelled—screamed, right. Damn.

I jolted up and looked around.

And I knew what was wrong.

Candy jumped back out of the bathroom.

"Jesus Christ, Todd, that fucking fish is in there!"

"What?" It—no, no way. But of course it was. I asked, "Candy?"

"You lied to me." Candy sat on the bed. "Fuck—I think I'm gonna be sick."

I got out of bed and stepped into the bathroom and looked into the toilet.

Aw, hell.

Candy said, "Fuck you, Todd."

I really sort of felt like vomiting, too. I looked into the toilet and poor dead Annette's head was sticking up out of the hole in the bottom, as if she was trying to swim back to the world of the living.

"Candy, I'm sorry," I said.

What the hell. What a goddamn disaster. I pushed the handle on the toilet and water poured out of the tank and swirled around the bowl, rising. Annette bobbed up and down as the water tried to get around her. She wriggled around like she was swimming—like she was fucking alive. The water slowly drained, trickling around the bobbing fish, and the level dropped in the bowl until it was back to normal. Still, the fish was stuck.

"Did it go?" Candy asked from the bedroom.

"Uh, no."

Candy said, "I asked you to do one thing for me."

I sat down on the edge of the tub and peered into the toilet. Annette was on her side, her eye, mouth, and gill plate sticking up. She looked alive.

"I'm getting out of here," Candy called.

"Yeah," I said. "Okay."

"Fuck you," Candy said. "Get it done."

I thought, I dropped her tail-first down the toilet, the spines on her dorsal fin must've caught on the pipe. Why didn't I think of that? Idiot. I reached into the toilet and grasped the fish by the head and pulled. Nothing happened. It was stuck.

What the hell.

I got down on my knees and kneeled over the bowl. It was clean, at least, pure shining white porcelain with a green fish looking up from the bottom. I grasped the fish with both hands and pulled. Stuck tight. I held tighter—squeezed the dead fish, stiff and the same time squishy, and I pulled again. The fish slipped a little, then suddenly came loose and I fell backwards and banged into a shelf and I let go of the dead fish. It landed on my bare chest.

"Aw, shit!" I slapped at the fish—grossed out, the awful cold wet dead thing touching me, all slimy—and I rolled away onto a rug.

I sat up. The green and white fish lay next to me on the pink rug, glistening. There were indentations on its side where I squeezed it, and its tail was curling up a little bit. I was ill, right—sick. I thought of the time when I was a kid and there were those dead rabbits on the back porch, still warm, with spots of blood showing where they had been shot, a flea or two jumping in their clean-smelling fur—I think I remember the fleas, I think I remember that they smelled like new hay, though maybe I'm making all that up, my memories all distorted by years of living and hearing that fucking stupid story told again and again, but still, in my mind they smelled fresh and new—and then my mother had come out and put the limp rabbits into a bucket and said that the rabbits were going away— the dead rabbits were going home!

Of course, you know what happened, right?

The stupidly obvious thing happened.

The next night we all ate the rabbits, we ate the rabbits, and of course I didn't know the difference—not, at least, until my parents told me, laughing and laughing and laughing—laughing, for years—at poor little me.

Saturn V

Just before we left to take our boy to the Cub Scout Space Fair, I found out that Bev was cheating on me. I found out: she told me so herself. I didn't know what to think—I still don't know what to think. It was numbing, really—I could barely think anything. I had no idea. I guess I'm pretty stupid. I sat on the couch while Bev went and made sure Richard was ready, and then they came out and the three of us got in the car and I drove—silently, slowly, cautiously, aware that my life had just changed for the worse, that something bad had happened—down to the United Methodist Church, where the monthly meeting and Space Fair was being held. I missed the parking lot and drove past the church and ended up pulling over about two blocks up the street. Bev looked at me but didn't say anything. We got out of the car and I stood there and I looked across the roof of the car at—Bev.

I asked, "So, why did you tell me about that?"

"Because I always tell you everything," Bev said. "I always do. I don't like being a liar."

That didn't make any sense.

"Why did we park so far away?" Richard asked.

"Be quiet," I said. I turned and walked quickly down the hill to the church.

At the meeting, I stood in the back of the room and watched everyone—all the other men, that is, the dads, wondering who Bev was sleeping with. There were sixty or so rowdy little boys with blue shirts and different kinds of space helmets running around and making noise, but I didn't focus on them. They weren't even a distraction. All he could think about was Bev. She didn't want to be a liar, okay, but still she hadn't told me—she actually refused to tell me—who she was sleeping with. And she always tells me everything, and she doesn't like to be a liar. Okay. Sure! And I believed that.

Sure.

It could have been anybody. Bev was sitting right in front of me on a metal folding chair, the kind of chair pro wrestlers hit each other over the head with, talking with some of the other moms, and every time I glanced down at the back of Bev's head I thought of hitting a few people over the head with a metal folding chair.

Starting with Bev.

"Are you okay?"

A voice—a question.

"Huh?" I looked around. It was Joan Jordan, Richard's Den Mother. Den 3—the Place to Be. She had dark eyes and looked worried.

"I asked if you're okay. You don't look so good."

"I guess I'm fine."

Joan frowned. She didn't believe me, and I looked away, suddenly embarrassed. I could see Richard, standing behind a table holding the rocket we'd built, the rocket I'd built—a big rocket, a Saturn V. The boy was chattering away to some other scouts. Showing off again. The boy bragged too much.

"Well, you don't look fine," Joan said after a moment. "Are you sick?"

Sick. For fuck's sake. I said, "No—I'm fine."

"Well, if you say so...."

I shrugged, sniffed, glanced at the back of Bev's head in front of me, and then—what the hell?—my heart skipped a beat. The pregnancy test! Fuck! I hadn't even thought of that until just now. A few weeks earlier Bev had been a bit late and had gotten frantic—almost hysterical—and nagged me out to make a midnight trip to the grocery store to buy a pregnancy testing kit. Her pee looked like Sprite. And when the color didn't change—when she finally came to believe the test—Bev had been so happy, almost giddy. We had a drink or two. We watched TV. We made love. Yeah! And all the time Bev of course had been thinking about—him. The other guy. Whoever the hell he was. She'd been afraid she was pregnant with his kid.

And, you know, now I really did want to hit her.

"What do you think of the space helmets?" Joan asked.

"What?" I looked back at Joan. Glared at her. I looked away. Didn't want to hit her. I said, "Oh—the space helmets. They're wonderful."

Bev turned around and looked at me. She whispered something to the mom sitting next to her, who laughed. My heart pounded. I took a breath.

"Really," I said. I forced myself to smile, and that was hard, a stiff smile. "They're great helmets. You must've put a lot of work into them, huh?"

Joan was raising her son by herself but always seemed to find time to do things, to be Den Mother, to do artsy-craftsy stuff. She'd made the helmets for the scouts of Den 3 out of empty plastic buckets, cutting out a panel and replacing it with clear plastic for a vision port, and installing little LED lights on the top.

"It wasn't that big a deal," Joan said. She looked over at Richard. "Richard's got the best rocket. I bet you sort of helped him with it a little, huh?"

"Well, no," I said.

The fucking rocket. For the goddamn Space Fair. The scouts were supposed to be celebrating "America's

Heritage of Space Exploration," but Richard had wanted to make something out of Star Wars. Something not real. And every time I explained the theme to him, he just shook his head. So I went ahead and built the rocket myself, and it was the best one there—better than all the space shuttles, international space stations, and Millennium Falcons that the other kids—or their dads or moms, more likely—had built.

I said, "I just sort of had the concept."

Joan nodded. "Of course."

Across the room, I saw a scout from Den 5 say something to Richard, and Richard handed the rocket across the table to him. The Den 5 kid was obviously impressed with it. I shook my head.

"Listen," Joan said. "I've got to go. I'll call you this week about the field trip."

Field trip. Whatever it was, wherever we were going. I'd forgotten about it.

"Okay," I said. "I'll talk to you later."

Joan squeezed my arm. "Take care of yourself, Jinx—really."

"Okay," I said. "Sure."

I watched her cross the room and say something to her little boy—Jacob, another scout, Richard's best friend—when I saw that Bev had turned around and was looking at me. She was smiling. Really, I felt like smacking her.

I asked, "What do you want?"

Bev said, "I don't want anything."

We went out, talking to a few people about nothing, the weather, the space fair, nothing, and then we were putting on our jackets in the church hallway, and almost alone, and Bev leaned over to me.

"You could be a little less obvious with Joan Jordan," she said.

"What?" I looked around, stepped closer to Bev. "What?"

"Joan," Bev said. "Typical way of getting back at me."

"You know there's—" Though now there was an idea, at least. Joan Jordan! I said, "Oh, just stop it."

Richard came bobbing up then, wearing his helmet, carrying the big white Saturn V in his arms. There was a red ribbon stuck to the rocket booster: a second place winner.

"Stop what?" Bev asked.

"Stop trying to make a fucking excuse for—" I thought for a moment. "For whatever you did."

"Everybody thought the rocket was great," Richard said.

I looked down at Richard. "Yeah, I saw everybody thinking it was great. I saw you showing off, too, acting like you built the whole goddamn thing by yourself."

Bev bent over and helped Richard put his jacket on—difficult, because he wouldn't take the rocket out of his arms. She looked up at me.

"Just stop," I said again. "Okay?"

Bev stood up and shook her head. Like she was disgusted with me. With me! She patted Richard on the back of his space helmet.

"C'mon, Richie, let's go home."

Outside it was cool and clear, and I walked silently up the hill to where the car was parked. I didn't have anything to say. Bev was quiet, too, walking with her hands in her pockets. But Richard was excited and babbling about the meeting.

"Everybody liked the rocket," he said. "They all wanted to see it."

"Yeah, I saw," I said. The boy talked too much sometimes, bragged. "I saw you behind that table going, 'This is mine, I built it! I built it!' Just showing off like everything."

Bev said, "Jinx, stop mocking him."

"I'm not mocking him—that's what he was saying."

"No, I wasn't showing off," Richard said. "I never told anybody I built it."

"Don't lie to me, Richard."

"I'm not—"

What I meant to do was give Richard a rap—a tap—sharp, but friendly—on the side of his hard plastic space helmet.

Really, that's what I meant to do.

But Richard turned just then to look at me—to say he wasn't a liar, I guess—and the back of my hand burst through the clear plastic and struck Richard on the mouth.

"Ow!" Richard dropped the rocket and put his hands over his face.

I just stood there.

I swear I didn't mean to hit him hard.

I mean, I was thinking about hitting Bev, hard—hitting her with a fucking chair—but I probably wouldn't even have done that.

So I just stood there.

Bev knelt down and pulled Richard's space helmet off and dropped it to the sidewalk. She pulled his hands away from his face.

She asked, "Are you okay?"

Richard bobbed his head—it was hard to tell if he bobbed it side-to-side no or up-and-down yes—and then he broke away from her took off running up the street to the car.

Bev picked the rocket off the sidewalk and stood, holding it under her arm. We looked at each other. Up the street Richard was standing outside the locked car.

"Way to go, Jinx," Bev said. "Way to fucking go."

It May Be a Day,
It May Be Forever

Every time the door opened and more people came into the bar a gust of cold air came blowing in behind them. I was sitting next to the door and I could feel the cold run all through me and I tell you now I liked it a lot better than I liked the people. They were all acting like it was something special just because it was New Year's—there were people playing pool, there were people talking and laughing, everybody was drunk, the bar was all smoky and noisy. They were all full of shit. I just wanted to sit at the bar and drink beer and feel cold. I just wanted to be left alone.

"Happy New Year, man," the guy next to me said when I looked around. He was black, young, a kid. He smiled and lifted his bottle at me.

"Go fuck yourself," I said.

He jolted back like he'd been slapped.

"Yeah, fuck you," I said. "Just leave me the fuck alone."

"Fuck you," he said. He was a wiry little guy, not much bigger than me. He was a junkie, maybe, or a drunk. Or maybe he just wanted to get his ass kicked. I was pretty well fucked up myself, so I didn't care.

"No, man, fuck you first, motherfucker." I shoved him off his stool. When he got his balance he came up to shove me but I was ready, had the knife out, and I stabbed up and in. It hit him on the top inside of his arm, in the bicep.

"Shit," I said. You always want to make your first shot a good one. The kid was stupid, though—he could've hit me with a bottle with his other hand, or he could've run away, or he could've done a lot of things, but he didn't do anything, he just stood there looking like a stupid fucking piece of shit.

I pulled out the knife and stabbed him in the chest. The pretty-boy bartender dropped a bottle and that was the first I knew that people were looking at me. The kid was just standing there.

I started to get pissed off.

I pulled out again and stuck the dumb fuck in his belly. Then I pulled up and ripped him open, gutted him like a fucking fish, and it made this great sound—ripping, tearing, not just his stupid red flannel shirt but his skin, too, his belly was opening up and his fucking guts were pouring out the gash and it all sounded like the end of the fucking world. He was the second or third or fourth guy I'd stabbed that night and the sound that came out of him was like nothing I'd ever heard before. My knife hit something hard and I could feel his insides pumping and the feeling tingled up my arm into me and I felt like it was my heart that was going to explode instead of his. It was like nothing I ever felt before, either, and I knew the piece of shit was going to die.

For a second or so I didn't know what to do. I took a breath and looked the black guy in his red eyes and he just looked surprised. It was like he couldn't see me, like I wasn't even there. He was as good as gone. I pulled on the knife with my tingling arm but it was stuck.

"Hey, hold it!"

It was hard to tear myself away from the kid, but I let go of the knife and turned around. Some other stupid fucking college kid in a blue shirt was standing there with a pool cue. A pretty big guy but he looked scared. I took two steps forward and punched the fucker good, right between the fucking eyes. I fucking coldcocked the cocksucker with my right hand. He took a step back and keeled over onto a table and then rolled to the floor and the table turned over too and there were all these bottles rolling around and breaking and I was happy because it was like we were in a fucking movie, a TV show, a western. I laughed.

I said, "Fuck you, cowboy."

I looked around and the dumbfuck I stabbed was still standing there, only now there was blood dribbling out his mouth. He had one hand on his chest and the other on a barstool. Blood was running from his belly down his pants and some yellow and gray shit, I guess it was his guts, was poking out around his stupid shirt.

"Hey, man, give me back my fucking knife." I put my hand on his shoulder—it was the first time I'd touched the stupid fuck and he felt all soft and trembly—and I grabbed the handle of the knife and pulled. I pulled hard and it came out slow. There were bits of red cloth and bloody crud on the blade and I wiped it off on my jacket.

"He's limp! Travis! He's limp!" I heard this from behind me. I guess Travis was the fucking cowboy with the pool cue. Good fucking deal. The asshole tried to fuck with me.

The bartender was still staring at me. He was scared shitless, he just stood there with his pretty hair and his mouth open like he was waiting for me to stick my dick in it.

"Don't fuck with me, man," I said.

He didn't say anything. I could hear cowboy Travis's friend talking to him. The stabbed guy was standing there, only now he was wobbling a little bit. My beer was still on the bar so I grabbed the bottle and took a long drink. I was really thirsty. There was a mirror behind the bar and

I looked in it and could see everybody in the bar looking back out at me. I could see me looking back out at me. I looked in the mirror and put the knife back in my jacket pocket.

I said, "So just don't fuck with me, okay?"

Nobody said anything. Nobody did anything. Nobody fucked with me. I finished the beer and pitched the bottle behind the bar and it smashed into some other bottles and that sounded good, too. Then I was out the door and the air was clear and cold and I was away from all those assholes.

I walked a couple of blocks down to the river and lit a cigarette. The city was lit up nice and it was cold and dark so there wasn't anybody around to bother me. You could hear sirens all over the city, though, and pops from bottlerockets and firecrackers going off for the New Year. I stood there smoking and after a while I saw a car on the other side of the river come around a corner and swerve and smash quietly into a building. Fucking drunks. I smiled and threw the butt into the grass by the river and I headed home.

My sister Berta was still up. She was sitting on the floor watching some stupid movie on TV and it smelled like she'd been smoking some weed. The house was hot. The lights were turned down and there was all this blue light from the TV and some flashing red lights from the Christmas tree in the corner. I could hear the gurgling from Mom's oxygen machine in the other room.

"Be quiet," she said. "Mom went to bed and Monica's asleep, too."

"Aw, fuck them," I said. I went on into the kitchen and got a beer.

"What's wrong with you?" Berta asked.

"Nothing." I came back into the living room and sat on the couch. I opened the beer and took a drink and it tasted good. I was still thirsty. My hand was sore and starting to swell up from where I'd punched the cowboy.

"You didn't go to Tommy's party?"

"Yeah, but it sucked. So then I went to some bars but there were all these fucking drunks around." I thought of the guy I'd stabbed, his red eyes.

"You should've stayed home," Berta said.

I was staring at the TV. This monster—or something, I guess it was a monster, this thing—that looked like a giant golf ball was chasing people around in the dark. Every time the Christmas tree flashed a static line jumped across the screen and it seemed like the people in the movie jumped, too.

"So what're you doing here, anyway?" I asked after a while. "Couldn't you get Mom to watch Monica?"

Berta turned around and looked at me. I couldn't see her face very well but all of a sudden she sounded mad.

"No, I couldn't," she said. "Somebody has to stay home and watch Mom, forget about Monica. And you were out fucking around so I had to stay in."

"Aw, fuck you." I was tired of fighting. It was probably a big mistake to come home but I didn't have anywhere else to go right then. Fucking home. How stupid.

"No, Jesse, fuck you. You're never any help with Mom, you're always off fucking around, you're—"

I threw the can of beer at her and it hit her in the face and bounced off squirting foamy white beer all over. It barely stunned her. Berta was quick. She was up off the floor and over the coffee table and on me almost before I could do anything. She caught me good in the eye with her right hand and grabbed my hair with her left. I squirmed away and hit her good with my sore right hand and got up off the couch. Berta was screaming. She got up and jumped at me again and hit me once or twice but I managed to turn her around and grab her by the tits and throw her back down on the couch. I sat down on her chest and hit her two or three times in the face but she kept on screaming.

"Wha—wha—what's this?"

I looked up and Mom was there in her wheelchair, oxygen tube running from her nose back out to her tank. She looked even grayer than normal in the light from the TV.

"Fuck you, Mom, this ain't none of your business."

"Call the cops!" Berta yelled. I put my hand over her mouth and she bit me.

"Bitch!" I hit her good.

"Jesse...." Mom gasped.

"Mom," I said. "Go back to bed. You just got out of the fucking hospital."

I got up off the couch and stepped onto the coffee table instead of over it but the piece of shit was made of wood and broke underneath me. I stumbled across the room to Mom.

"This is all your fucking fault, okay?" I said. "So just get the fuck back to bed."

"I...I...I...." Mom made noises like the air going out of a big balloon. It sounded like she was never going to stop so I kicked the side of her wheelchair.

"Shut up! Go back to bed! This all your fucking fault!" I shook my fist at her. I kicked her chair once more but I guess I kicked too hard because the wheelchair went over and Mom rolled out onto the floor and she looked up at me scared.

"You think I asked for this shit? Huh? You think I want to live with you fuckers? You think I fucking asked to be fucking born? Fuck you, this is all your fucking fault, you fucking bitch!"

Then I saw something move out of the corner of my eye and before I could jump there was a fucking huge explosion in my shoulder and it really, really fucking hurt—I was seeing fucking stars and I didn't even get hit in the head. I went down.

It was Berta. She'd snuck around to the closet and gotten my softball bat, a big gold aluminum 36-ounce Worth Ball Buster, and she'd hit me with the fucker. Bitch.

Berta was a pretty good ball-player and had a good swing but I managed to roll away before she hit me again.

"Shit!" I scrambled back across the floor and got up.

"Don't fuck with Mom!" Berta was waving the bat like she was waiting for a good pitch to come across the plate.

"Fuck you!"

She faked a swing and I fell for it and then there she was with the real thing and it caught me in the same spot on my shoulder, only not as hard. I stumbled back against the TV and knocked it over and the fucker sort of exploded or shattered or crashed or something with sparks and smoke and then the only light in the room was coming from the damn flashing Christmas tree. Berta swung again and I jumped back and knocked the tree over and some of the balls popped when they broke on the floor. The lights stayed on, though. Mom was on the floor gasping and then I could hear little Monica crying. I took another step back.

"I'm sick of your shit, Jesse."

Berta still had that fucking bat. I could see her when the red lights flashed. She swung but missed because the tree was between us and then she swung again and got me on the arm. This time, though, I was ready and I grabbed the head of the bat. I got it with both hands and jumped over the tree at her. Berta had a better grip on the handle but I was stronger than her even though my shoulder was fucked up.

We spun around the room trying to get the bat away from each other and then Berta slammed into a door frame and let go. I got the handle of the bat and clubbed her hard on the knee and she went down with a scream.

"Fucking bitch!" I yelled. "What the fuck are you do-ing?"

I kicked her four or five times where her balls would've been if she'd had any. Then I stepped back and caught my breath. I was leaning on the bat. Little Monica came into the room and ran across the floor to Berta.

Monica was crying and Berta and Mom sounded about the same, both gasping for air.

"Shit!" I said. "What the fuck is wrong with you people? Are you all fucking crazy?"

I threw the bat across the room. It smacked into the wall and the head stuck in the plaster. For a moment the whole bat stuck out from the wall and then it tilted down and fell to the floor.

"Jesus, you people are really fucked up, man, you know that? You're fucked!"

I walked to the door and left the house. That was just one more stupid kind of thing to do, I guess, because I really didn't have any place else to go. I just wanted to get away from those people. I walked a couple of blocks down the street and stood under a streetlight and lit a cigarette. I was pretty banged up—my face hurt, my hand hurt, my arm hurt, my shoulder really fucking hurt. Fucking Berta could fight.

I finished the cigarette and took a breath and headed on downtown. I didn't have anything else to do. I don't know why this kind of shit happens to me. All I know is it was a really fucked way to start a New Year.

The Road Back
to Wherever

Like all vacations, my stay in the hospital came to an end. After thirteen days they let me go. Dr. Jamail gave me a big bag of charity meds and told me not to be so lazy. The hot nurse told me to live my life like a lion. The heart attack guy didn't say anything—I think he resented me as much as I resented him.

Katy walked me out of the hospital and drove me back to my apartment. My roommate was worried about how we were going to pay the electric bill. A day later I was back in the cab, driving a 24-hour shift, driving here, driving there, in the days hot hard sunlight reflected and glaring off of cars and buildings, at night all neon and shadows—driving, trying to keep my fantasies alive, trying to convince myself that I was actually driving somewhere I wanted to go. That I had a destination. I tried to convince myself that the people sitting behind me in the cab had something to say—I listened to their stories, I tried to understand their lives, I tried to live their lives, I tried to be not me. But it didn't work. Nothing worked. I grew more and more frazzled. Nothing made me happy.

So, in the end, I just drove and drove and drove, and then I decided to talk.

Acknowledgments

Thanks to all the many good people who helped: Andrea Bates, Patricia Bjorklund, Pamela Booton, Olivia Burgess, Chris Carmona, Florence Davies, Ken Fontenot, Phil Gavenda, Morgan Gross, Alysa Hayes, Larry Heinemann, Kathryn Lane, Jerome Loving, Janet McCann, Skip Morris, Chuck Taylor, Reji Thomas, Javier VanWisse-Booton, Sienna Ward, Diane Wilson, Sara Zachry. And special thanks to the students of ENGL 451, who offered helpful advice and inspiration: Shannon Ahlstedt, Scott Eberting, Marisa Hunn, Tiffany Krause, Zach Mitchell, Jessica Parke, Kristy Walker.

✷

Some of these stories have been previously published....

Callaloo: "The Road Back to Destruction Bay" (and, sort of, "The Road Back to Wherever") | *Concho River Review*: "Cassie's Shirt (as "Cindy's Shirt") | *Broken Bridge Review*: "The Quiet Sport" | *Amarillo Bay*: "Something Else Finally Happened" | *Blood Lotus Journal*: "Saturn V" (as

"Rocket") | *Cerebration*: "The Point" | *R-KV-R-Y*: "Deep Eddy" | *Prism Quarterly*: "Corky the Squirrel" | *Dominion Review*: "After the Sudden Garage Sale I Decided to Move to Texas" (as "How Much for All This?") | *Aethlon*: "The Endless Inning" | *Culture Concrete*: "It May Be a Day, It May Be Forever"

About Lowell Mick White

Lowell Mick White is the author of seven books: novels *Normal School* and *Professed* and *Burnt House* and *That Demon Life*, the story collections *Long Time Ago Good* and *The Messes We Make of Our Lives*, and the creative writing text *Answers Without Questions*. A winner of the Dobie-Paisano Fellowship and a member of the Texas Institute of Letters, White received his PhD from Texas A&M University.

Contact Lowell Mick White at www.lowellmickwhite.com